2 —

A LAZY EYE

STORIES

Mary Morrissy

SCRIBNER

SCRIBNER
1230 Avenue of the Americas
New York, NY 10020

First Scribner edition 1996
Originally published in Great Britain by Jonathan Cape.

SCRIBNER and design are trademarks of
Simon & Schuster Inc.

Manufactured in the United States of America

1 3 5 7 9 10 8 6 4 2

Library of Congress Cataloging-in-Publication Data
Morrissy, Mary, date.
A lazy eye : stories / Mary Morrissy.
p. cm
I. Title.
[PR6063.O7976L39 1996]
823'.914—dc20   96-18357
CIP

ISBN 0-684-19668-9

In memory of my father

CONTENTS

BOOKWORM

WHEN I WAS at school you could buy a black baby. The images of those hollow-eyed, skeletal children, flies on their eyelids, the mortifying protuberances of their wrist and ankle bones were part of our growing up. In our darkened classroom, captives of the mote-flecked beam, they stole over the familiar contours of blackboard and crucifix to the drowsy whir of the projector. When the blinds were lifted with a disconcerting snap, the nun would pass around a white, wooden collection box, a smiling black cherub squatting on the top. The thud of our coppers – ah, coins of nostalgia – made them seem distant already, as if they had started their journey to parched lands. And, sure enough, some months later, we would see more pictures. Different children this time, flashing broad white grins, happy in ill-fitting cast-offs, gathered outside crude schoolhouses or beside village wells. Their faces pressed up eagerly close to the lens as if to convince us that our pennies had bought their smiles.

Sometimes a nun newly returned from 'the missions' would talk over the slides. Always dressed in white creaseless cotton, these nuns stood out in every way against the dour serge we were used to. They were young,

3

animated. They talked to us, almost blamefully, of these children, of their hunger for learning, of how they sat barefoot at pitted wooden forms, inherited from the more privileged, engraved with hearts, names and messages, all foreign to them. Or of how they lustily sang *our* hymns which we merely mouthed. I imagined their voices to be harsh and clear like the light which suffused each picture of their homeland – as if the sun itself had lodged in their throats. There seemed to be a purity, a simplicity in their lives which we were to be forever denied.

I was reminded of them again when I saw this child in the bookshop. She was about four or five years old. She was not black, more the smooth honeyed colour of a half-caste. Her tightly fuzzed hair seemed grizzled in the artificial light. I half-expected her to be barefoot, but it was winter after all, and she was muffled up in a grey duffel coat. She wore a stout pair of brown, lace-up boots, oddly old-fashioned, the sort you see children wearing in ageing sepia photographs. Her socks, a bright canary yellow, were rumpled around her tawny ankles, falling over the edges of the boots like some tropical throw-back. Two golden studs pouted in her tiny ear lobes. She was singing in that seemingly absent-minded, but strangely concentrated way that children do, repeating the same phrase monotonously until you long to supply the cadence. She was wandering up and down between the shelves, one hand extended, so that sometimes

her finger would catch at the corner of a paperback, sending it clattering to the floor or else curling the cover
slightly leaving a vague crease. This might annoy you if
you were fond of books. I know some people who won't
lend books in case you spill tea or drop cigarette ash on
them, or bend down the right-hand corner of the pages
to mark how far you've read. Or, worst of all crimes,
turn them face down, fracturing the spines. Since I have
no respect for books, these things do not worry me. You
might think that strange since I have spent so much time
stealing books. But it is just that sepulchral atmosphere in
bookshops that makes them an easy target. It is presumed
that if you go into a bookshop that you must love all that
shiny merchandise, the glossy sheen of newly-published
paperbacks, their pages sticking together with newness.
You see them, these book lovers, caressing the stippled
covers of hardbacks or running their pale fingers over
colour plates. Sickening. That's why I liked this child.
She showed the same disdain for them as I did.

I started off in the clothing trade, favouring large department stores with communal dressing rooms. I would
choose two or three items, shirts or skirts, and neglect
to take one of them off, putting my own clothes on over
it. But then they started issuing little plastic counters for
each item or using those white lug-like attachments,
drooping from the clothes as blameless as the ears of a
cocker spaniel, but which set off a frenzied bleeping at
the door when you tried to take them out.

Anyway, I had grown tired of all those mirrors, and the sadness of seeing women disrobe revealing tired underwear, flesh-coloured bras, unseemly rolls of flesh and puckered elbows, and always, a light film of sweat on their brows. Their own clothes, sloughed from them, lay crumpled on the floor while they preened themselves before the mirrors – going up close, then retreating, flattening bulging bellies, pivoting around to profile and sweeping their hair high up on their heads in a strangely voluptuous manner, as if to lend grace to the outfit. But that was impossible. How could those rows and rows of corduroy and gaberdine be anything but graceless in the end? I recall with a shudder the flimsy polyesters, which gave off a tinselled static, as if something small and defenceless had been skinned in its making, leaving only a faint, silvered echo of its screams. Even the bright, floral cottons, with their great splashes of scarlet and magenta, seemed to languish in the fevered jungle heat.

No, bookshops are so restful in comparison, and much more hopeful. You can feel the bristling energy of hope rising off the books. All those authors earnestly offering themselves, in slim little packages, crying out for recognition from people like me. I wonder what it is like for *them* to walk into a bookshop and see slivers of themselves as if a surgeon had peeled off a section of their skin, bottled it, labelled it and set it on a shelf with a price. You're imagining already that I'm one of them, a disgruntled writer never rewarded, wreaking her revenge. Not so, I have never written in my life except for this dictated effort which will be counter-signed at the bottom by a guardian-of-the-law. You are asking for reasons, motives, as he is, as the psychiatrist will when he is called at the court hearing to explain my aberration. No one, you see, can accept blamefulness these days. A disturbed childhood, he will say, the crushing pressure to perform academically, the failed university career. Ah yes, he will nod understandingly, your father, the authoritarian figure with the scant education – 'sure I only went to the hedge school' – who both revered and despised books. I remember him, a big, ruddy-faced man with strangely trusting brown eyes, thumbing through my schoolbooks, plucking phrases from them like a magpie, and repeating them until he had beaten them senseless. And there was my mother who devoured romantic novels, borrowed from the library, encased in grubby plastic covers and printed in insultingly large print for the short-sighted. She became like the other bent old ladies we used to see at the library, who shuffled between the shelves, white-haired and slack-jawed, holding the books to their dry bosoms as if they were scented bouquets.

The library incident will of course be dragged up. How at seventeen, I invaded the local library, a municipal, red-bricked edifice, courtesy of Andrew Carnegie, which squatted on the high street under the shadow of the town hall clock. I walked up the polished wooden staircase and into the reading room. The door swung closed behind me and I went up to the desk. It was as hushed as a church. All those bowed heads and the faint rustle of paper, the odd agitated cough smuggled through the imposed silence. I felt I had stumbled into a meeting of a secret sect there in that high room, squares of pale winter sky conspiring at the windows. I would not have been surprised to find incense hanging in the air. There they sat, these pale monsters, supplicant, awaiting some kind of proclamation. 'She asked for information about beetles,' the short fat girl behind the counter would explain to my mother who was called to haul me away. 'I turned to look up the index and she just went berserk, sweeping her way through the shelves, flailing at the books, knocking them onto the ground . . . she was shouting, it was very disturbing. They are students here, not used to this sort of thing.'

I remember her outraged little face to this day, the wounded tone of her voice, her fingers clutching the worn edge of the desk. Sacrilege was the word on her lips.

She was wrong about the beetles. It was lice I was after, the humble booklice, or *psocoptera*, to give them their proper name. Wingless, they live indoors among old books and papers feeding on traces of mould. There is a whole army of them, well over a thousand species, gnawing the binding – they are partial to the paste – and piercing the pages of books with small holes. Having worked undisturbed for centuries, they were finally 'discovered' in 1701 when their ticking was traced to source in an English library. I am fond of such small industrious creatures – like the spiders who live in my bathroom. There are at least three of them, one permanently camped on the methyl green stain left by a tirelessly dripping tap. The other two, more social beings, snooze on the nether slopes of the enamel. I often sit on the bowl and watch them. They fight sometimes or perhaps it is some elaborate form of foreplay. Their tiny legs toy with one another, then lock in a vicious embrace. And then they part, retreating to resume their watchful torpor, lying motionless for hours. They disappear inexplicably for days, leaving the bath unembroidered. I often wonder what sprees they go on while they are away.

The spiders drove the last tenant out. She was terrified of them, and as if sensing her terror, they played malevolent tricks on her, lodging themselves under the light switch so her fingers would brush against their spongy bodies in the dark. She would run out into the hallway, hysterical, the neighbours tell me.

I like the squalor of the place. It is an old Georgian house, subdivided now, with sloping floors as if the mason who built it had been drunk or one-eyed. I prefer to think the structure has sagged in sympathy with those who tenant it. Even the rooms are lopsided, large windows squinting at both sides of thin partition walls, light bulbs dangling way off-centre, stucco work breached in midstream. The house overlooks the canal which is completely frozen over now. Winter dredges up the underworld debris. The rusty carcasses of cookers, cars, beds pierce the surface, always upended, Alp-like and ghostly. When it thaws they are submerged again, their season over.

My flat, of course, will throw more light on my activities. Like the tabloid image of suburban murder (the red-bricked house harbouring a grisly secret – a dismembered body, a bloodied hatchet?) the tools of my trade are innocuous enough – scissors and a blender. With the clothes there was no ritual of destruction. I tried hacking them with scissors or renting them with my bare hands, but they resisted. And, anyway, they looked more pathetic in their ragged pieces, they had more power over me. But there was mastery in destroying the books. I would first tear off the covers, then rip the pages out in clumps. I would cut each page into long thin strips and feed them to the blender. When they emerged they were like Michaelmas-daisies. I would stow them away in large plastic bags and weekly, I would leave the shredded offerings down on the street below, to be collected by dustmen. They would lie there beside the other bulging bags of tins, cartons, uneaten dinners and soggy tea-leaves. My bags were pristine, clean, as pure as a child in a christening robe. I would imagine their journey, mangled and crushed in the grinding, toothed lorry, smeared with the wretched saliva of household refuse, to be tipped out at the large dump by an angry, white-capped sea. Perhaps one or two pieces would remain unsullied, only to be haggled over by peevish seagulls, themselves the only white, clear beings on a landscape of greying, disintegrating humanity.

If that doesn't provide them with explanations, they may turn to my politics, looking under my mattress for subversive literature. A socialist, perhaps, they will think, indulging in a warped attack on materialism. Maybe. I once visited Moscow (more evidence) but all I remember are the vegetable stores, miles of shelves filled with cabbages, every one the same, and yet the housewives mulled and hesitated, feeling this one and that, weighing one against the other, as if *their* choice would make a difference.

It is all vanity. My vanity was to look too long at a prissed-up, coloured child in stout boots with a coarse accent and a jabbing, accusing finger. 'Mammy, mammy, look at her, look, she's taking them books.' And there I was, admiring the exotic and imagining it untouched. I hesitated – the downfall of the kleptomaniac – allowing the image of her sturdy, lithe limbs and the dark pools of her eyes to capture me.

POSSIBILITIES

AT FORTY-ONE, Grace Davey's biggest fear was that she would dry up. When she rose in the morning she would be relieved and delighted to find her loins pleasingly damp. The milky secretion of mid-cycle was a cause for secret celebration. So, when she discovered the greenish discharge she was not at all alarmed. It reminded her of the sap that oozes from the barks of pine trees – strong, pungent, fertile. The workings of her own body were a mystery to her. She took great trouble with her appearance. Her chestnut hair, streaked here and there with grey, was swept back in a coil from her lightly lined face and pale green eyes. She had a slender neck, graceful shoulders, girlish hips. Yet of her innards she had only the vaguest notion – an impression of oiled, livid organs performing languid, primitive rituals unquestioningly – which was why the discharge did not at first bother her. She certainly didn't relate it to Lucas. Her body was merely dispelling something nasty and sharp-smelling which it needed to get rid of. She bowed to its wisdom.

She took to bathing more often, aware that the acrid odours of one's own body are always more pleasing to oneself than others. She dabbed lavender water on her wrists and behind her ears to distract attention. But as the weeks wore on she would panic if anyone so much as wrinkled a nose in her presence. Once, on a particularly muggy day in late August, Mr Weatherby paused in the middle of dictation and started sniffing noisily. 'Don't you get it?' he asked rising from the desk and wandering around the room.

His penthouse office was all glass, the smoky tinted kind which threw a bronzed blanket on the sky and over the city far below. The air conditioner was whirring noisily but the room was still stuffy.

'Get what?' she asked sliding her hand furtively into her handbag for the lavender water.

'That smell. Like seaweed, rotting seaweed.'

Grace sat in a damp pool.

'Perhaps it's the river,' she suggested, willing him to move away. He was poised like a hound. She was afraid he would catch the smell of fear from her which was now stronger than the other smell. 'It was at low tide this morning and it always stinks in the summer.'

He paced up and down in his glassy cage. He was a small, soft man with the contours of a baby. A paunch, a soft, sagging chin, plum-like hands as if knuckles had never formed.

'You must be right,' he said, 'it looks pretty foul from here with all that greenish stuff clinging to the banks. Ugh, disgusting . . . !'

He stretched up and fiddled with the knob on the

air-conditioning box. Then he thumped it impatiently.

'Damn thing isn't worth a jot!'

Grace sighed with relief.

Lucas Spalding's hand appeared first through the hatch. Next came a head with dark, spiky hair, then a bare spindly torso. He had the sort of looks that until a certain age seem handsome and then suddenly become malevolent – when a dark eye turns beady, an arched eyebrow becomes demonic and a strand of brilliantined hair or tufts escaping from the nostrils seem like small fragments of evil. He hauled himself out on to the deck of the barge and sat with his legs clad in a shiny pair of dark pants dangling over the edge. He scratched his stubbly chin irritably and yawned. It was midday. He surveyed his world. The bridge forming a surprised O with its counterpart in the still, scummy water, the juggled backsides of houses on the far bank, the stone wall along the tow path with little back doors set into it and dark, glabrous ivy clinging to its crevices. On the near bank, a heap of rusting junk – an old-fashioned mangle, an upended wheelbarrow, a gaping cast-iron fireplace, all sprouting great, green tufts of weeds.

Like everything else in his life, Lucas had come upon this home by chance. The dilapidated barge had lain idle on the canal for years. It had been there for so long that it had become part of the geography of the place. The sight of its rust-red gangrenous hull sinking into the water would have been missed as much as the elm trees on the banks, were they to be felled. Lucas had moved in stealthily and taken possession. He knew how to insinuate himself into other people's lives; his trade required it. He had once worked in a photographic laboratory developing holiday snaps. He had seen it all there. Ugly, naked pendulous men smiling barefacedly at the camera; fat women splayed on bedspreads showing off bluish, mottled bottoms. People assumed that only a machine shared their tacky secrets, but they were wrong. Lucas Spalding knew them too. Sometimes, by chance, he would pass those same people on the street and he would flash a viperish grin at them. They often mistook his glee for friendliness and would wave gaily, if uncertainly, back at him as if he were someone they had met at a party and couldn't quite put a name to. But, in fact, it was the other way round. He worked now only when he had to. When he was short of cash he would take his camera down to the Merchants Bridge in the city. He wore a sign around his neck which read 'INSTANT PHOTOS'. The summer season was the best. The heat drove people to all sorts of vanity. The trick was to stop them as they linked one another across the bridge – usually young couples in the first flush of romance – and offer them something to remember their night by. The funny thing was that they were always flattered to be chosen, not realising that he chose them for one reason only, that they were easy prey. Suckers!

It was on the bridge that he had met Grace on a

warm, thundery summer's night. The sky was a deep inky blue. She approached wearing a pale raincoat which flapped accommodatingly to show a lozenge of floral thigh. He did not usually stop lone women; they were either sullen or scathing and were not likely to buy. But there was something in her buoyant stride, her hair and coat afloat like one of those young girls on bicycles, that dared to be interrupted.

'Photo Madam?' he called out, bowing into her path.

She came to such a quick halt that his temple brushed against her breast as he straightened himself. He quivered. Quickly he drew a chipped mirror from his breast pocket. For the undecided this was usually the clincher. They rarely resisted this ritual presentation of their own image. She did not demur. Lucas brushed a stray hair from her cheek. Then, catching her firmly by the shoulder, he guided her back to the spot where he had first seen her. Holding the camera close to his chest he beckoned to her with a grubby hand. She walked towards him. His coat billowed around him as he reversed. A ghostly blue flash went zig-zagging between feet and legs and into the silent shadows of the river below. Minutes later the wet print came lolling out of the camera, black at first, then grey and cloudy before finally clearing into a bright exposure. She took the print, still damp, and held it delicately by its edges. The flash had made her chestnut hair seem brighter, her smile more moist, the blue night more electric.

'So, this is how I look,' she said.

'The camera never lies,' he replied.

Suddenly a large drop of rain fell on the print like a fat childish tear. The trees rustled in a fit of restlessness. Thunder rumbled in the sky. Lucas looked up.

'Better shelter, there's going to be an almighty down-pour,' he said, touching her fleetingly in the small of her back.

'Look, over there . . . '

He grasped her hand. She ran along beside him feeling suddenly girlish, her light summer shoes clacking on the pavement. They tumbled into a doorway. There was already a crowd there, huddled together mournfully watching the shower. Arrows of rain lanced the kerbside puddles. A gutter nearby streamed blue and gold. In the crush she found herself pressed up against him but even when the rain had eased and the other people had gingerly ventured out, Lucas and Grace still stood close together, their warm damp breaths mingling, their fingertips just touching.

There were many things Grace liked about Lucas. He had the smell of a farmer, milky and slightly rancid. There was grit beneath his nails and a dirty rim around his neck. The collars of his shirts were frayed. She liked these things because she knew they would never have to be accommodated. For Grace the word 'we' was a strange and impossible notion. There had been other men, of course, but always unsuitable. There were some people whom one couldn't accommodate in one's life, she had discovered, who just wouldn't fit in. Like the lame carpenter she had been seeing who squirmed in company and could only talk about joists and dovetails. She had found men's need for closeness irksome; she did not want to be troubled by their small grievances and petty outrages. And it was easy, so easy, to embarrass Grace. She had a finely tuned sense of embarrassment which, at times, was as acute as physical pain. It was to this that the men before Lucas had fallen prey.

Grace visited the barge three times a week. Lucas would wait for her in the dark. There were rarely any preliminaries. He would light the little gas bracket and put the kettle on the stove. By the time it had boiled Lucas would have already come. Sometimes there would not even be time to take their clothes off so that they would end up in odd states of dishevelment, Lucas with his pants round his ankles, Grace with a breast exposed above a strangled bra. They would smile gratefully at one another with wet teeth and swollen mouths, without the slightest hint of foolishness. He called her Gracie. She was surprised to find it neither bleak nor dispiriting. Lucas was the only man who had ever made her feel wanton. Once he asked her to come to the barge with as few clothes on as possible. She travelled on the train wearing only a raincoat, buttoned and belted, but the thought that she was naked underneath drove her to such excitement that Lucas's first touch produced a wet spasm of sheer delight.

'There's nothing like it,' he would say, 'pure sex.'

Grace was inclined to agree. Afterwards she would dress and settle her hair while Lucas made tea. They would sit by the stove sipping from enamel mugs, snug as a pair of pensioners. He never pleaded with her to stay. They were as wary of one another's territory as a pair of animals might have been. Nightly, Grace returned to her scented bed while Lucas rearranged the divan and fell asleep in a nest of blankets which bore the tart smell of their union. And if she passed Lucas on the bridge the only acknowledgement between them was the flutter of an eyelid and that anarchic sense of conspiracy that accompanies any act of intimacy between two people.

It was only when the sores appeared that Grace began to worry. She went to the clinic. She was issued with a number and told to wait in the crowded waiting room. She could feel her cheeks burning with shame. She fixed her eyes on the floor and studied the creases in her shoes. Nobody spoke and the only time a head was raised was when the door to the surgery opened and a new number was called.

He was a young doctor with sandy hair and an air of discreet disappointment. And why not, Grace thought. Her kind of illness was a failing, after all. It showed an absence of care and good taste. The treatment, he reassured her, was a hundred per cent effective. It would, of course, mean abstinence for some time, but in a monogamous relationship like hers, some accommodation could surely be made. Of course, there might be some side-effects, he went on. Nothing dramatic, no facial hair or anything like that. But she might notice a certain dryness – in the vaginal area. Absolutely nothing to worry about. Most women were actually quite glad of it, he said. He fixed her with a candid gaze.

'The main thing,' he said, 'is to cut down on the possibilities, to ensure that this sort of thing doesn't happen again . . .'

ROSA

FROM HIS PALACE in Rome the Pope had ordered a holy year. Everyone in our small city was touched. Even Penbridges, the big department store where I work, had pushed Santa Claus to one side. Usually he holds the centre stage in the large foyer on the first floor, sitting beneath a great, needle-dropping tree, its branches laden down with silvered, snowy baubles. This year he was huddled in one corner while in the centre was a huge crib with life-size figures. The management had even considered having real animals, a donkey and an ox, nuzzling close to the child, but they couldn't risk the possibility of steaming turds on the carpet so they settled for plaster-cast models of the animals instead. But the *pièce-de-résistance* was the baby, a black baby. It was a stroke of genius. We rarely see a dark face in these parts and so it seemed Penbridges had absolved all our prejudices with one bold gesture.

It was Rosa who pointed this out to me. Rosa is my sister, younger than me by five years although it has never seemed that way. I live on the edges of her dark, livid world until it seems that without her I would barely exist, that I would be a mere spectre, passing in and out unseen through the sullen doorways of her life. Even her name, Rosa, is a sort of concoction. At home we used to call her Rosie – a dark, freckled child squatting in patches of mud or clumps of grass, burrowing with her tiny, dimpled hands. When she came to the city she became Rosa, conjuring up an image of deep, sultry eyes and a small, fluid body. And in time she became that, as if, chameleon-like, her wish was enough to create.

In the last months of her confinement she visited Penbridges' crib daily. Then, I dismissed these trips as just another vagary of pregnancy like the early cravings for pineapple and raw meat. And I thought perhaps this, the ultimate picture of maternity, was actually taking hold of her. It was, at least, warm and safer there than the crowded, wet streets which she tramped constantly. She would come back to our rooms barefoot, soaked through, her hair wringing, her sodden shoes in her hand, their dye leaving faint red patches in the hollows beneath her ankle bones. But in Penbridges she made quite a pious picture, a heavily pregnant girl kneeling before the crib, tinselled angels hanging above her, little scrolls emanating from their trumpets with Gothic-red messages emblazoned on them. Oh, they had got everything right – the melting snow on the roof, the obsequious hunch of the shepherds, the stained wooden slats of the manger, even the acrid smell of the stable. But to me it reeked of artifice; all this elaborate effort to create an imitation.

'Look,' Rosa said to me when we went there together. 'Look at Joseph and Mary, how pale they are. They don't seem a bit put out that the baby is a different colour.' She cackled. 'That's religion for you . . . '

He was like a cat, fleeting in moonlight. I heard them thrashing in the night, then the sudden, shocked stillness of their union. Did I imagine a coldness in their pleasure? Perhaps. But, like the crib, it was a fine imitation. I watched them as one might trace with a finger the gentle lashing of fish against the glass of an aquarium. When he was gone she would sit with her back to me, her lips suppressed with a kind of excitement. I would stand behind her, one hand in hers, the other settled in the sad curve of her neck parting the tiny strands of hair with my thumb until I had laid bare her forlorn nape and her bridled fervour had melted away into a sated melancholy. I knew, of course, that he would abandon her, and I simply waited. And, sure enough, one evening I heard him fleeing, down the stone flights and through the landings below, the clatter of his footsteps fading like the tinny jubilance of an empty vessel hurled into the depths of a well.

We were left to count the days. The pale squares of the calendar seemed to grow hollow-eyed from our attention. Every morning I sought tell-tale signs on her white underwear but it yielded up only the indolent smell of sex which clung to her long after he was gone. Rosa grew strangely listless. When we went to the clinic she held my hand, placing herself trustingly in my care. We sat silent as a haggard woman with skin like suede and a soothered child on her lap addressed the waiting-room.

'Never had any trouble with the other three, but this one has my heart broke. Always sick, always cranky . . . '

The child sat, stoppered and somehow accusing. I winked and smiled at her, believing that such clownish behaviour was expected, but she stared back, unblinking, solemn.

As we went home, Rosa glanced at her newly confirmed shape in shop windows. Serpentine mannequins, their fingers arched mockingly like Balinese dancers, their heads tilted quizzically, smiled back at her. She stopped once, staring through them at her own reflection.

'It's not really there,' she said, flattening her stomach.

'Rosa, Rosa . . . '

'It's like a balloon . . . I could easily burst it.'

'Rosa, we are not murderers.'

And, even if we were, who would have helped us in a year when vigils were held at grottoes and rosaries were broadcast in railway stations?

'We must tell Father,' I said.

The thought of going home filled us both with dread, not for what we had to tell him, but for the mastery of his dismal existence over us. He has been alone for years, ever since Mother died in childbirth with our stillborn brother. Now he shuffles around our dark little cottage, swamped by moss-coloured clothes. Crumbs of cigarette ash settle on the sheeny crotch of his pants as he sits by the dim glow in the grate. He runs a crinkled hand through his thick,

grey strands which are as coarse as horse hair, and sighs.
It is not great unhappiness. No, it is as if he expected this
grim ebb-tide in his life and is mesmerised by its seething
undertow.

It was I, in the end, who told him while Rosa sat in the
overgrown garden, idly plaiting her hair. He shifted once
in his chair but said nothing. I knew then that nothing we
did or said could ripple the hypnotic stillness of his own
gloom. But, as we were leaving, he caught me roughly
by the arm and said with a sagging smile, 'She has won
you over, our little Rosa.' Was it then I passed over into
Rosa's world? No, even then, there were corners of it
into which she retreated that I could only guess at. Once
I found a half-empty bottle of gin in the bathroom and
a rim of grime around the tub where she had lain for
hours. Another time she tried to prick the surface of her
belly with a safety pin as if to tear it open, until I prised
the pin from her hand.

I used to bring her gifts from the outside world
– small, strawberry-filled chocolates, a pink velvet rib-
bon for her hair, a bright crimson dress. I brought her
books, manuals of motherhood full of tranquil passages
and soft photographs of swollen women, but she only
pointed to the protective male hands on each of their
bellies as if I were trying to taunt her. I remember the
rolling gait of two, her arms encompassing the bump
in a gesture of aborted protection. When we passed
blooming, bulbous girls on the street she would point

after them. 'Dromedaries, one-humped camels, beasts of burden, that's all we are.' And yet, she had never looked healthier. Abandonment had given her a luring, almost sexual glow.

But sometimes, late at night, I would hear her softly whimpering in her sleep. Once she woke in terror crying, 'How will it come out?' as mind overtook body in the nine-month race. The thumping being beat in her like a drum, she said, resenting its confinement, the distended part so ugly now, displacing all her innards, leeching energy, dictating. I had no answers, but held her head in my lap until she went back to sleep. In time, her body answered for her, flexing its muscles, preparing regardless, tightening, clenching around its prize, her skin stretched to translucence. Full-blown, circumferenced, we awaited the eruption.

I could not be with her for the birth. The week before Christmas is Penbridges' busiest time and I had to report for work as usual. I was on Cold Cuts in the food hall, sawing through flaky breasts of chickens or using the slicer on sweating joints of ham. While Rosa lay somewhere else on a cold slab, the midwife in a butcher's apron, the nurses gathered around like spectators at a bullfight, their urgent cries mixing with hers of pain. As I passed cold, wet bags of giblets across the counter, there might be a great tearing of skin . . . The doctor would hold the balloon up, a small, shrivelled thing. It would hang there for a moment, then he would pass it to her. And Rosa would catch it up by its slim neck and put it to her lips. At first it might make no move – then it would leap, salmon-like, into life. Or would she just gently let it go, releasing her fingers from its slender neck, and watch it shudder and recede . . . I longed to be with her.

The store did not close until nine. I walked home through the soiled, littered streets thinking only of her. On my way I bought flowers. Not roses because she said they reminded her of death, but speckled orange tiger lilies. She was standing on the doorstep when I arrived, the baby muffled in her arms.

'Rosa, what's happened?'

She put her finger to her lips and motioned for us to go in. We made our way up the stairways, slowly, because her stitches were still raw and broke her tread. Beneath her coat I could see a hospital shift. Her feet were in slippers and her hair at the back was clotted with sweat. No one passed us. When we got to our rooms, we pulled out a drawer from the dresser, lined it with a soft blanket and placed the child in it. I lit a fire (the room was icy) and made some broth. We sat for hours saying nothing, until I could bear the imposition of her silence no longer.

'You want to get rid of it, don't you?'

She nodded like a child being coaxed out of a sulk.

'But how? Where?'

'We'll leave it in the crib.'

We rose early on Christmas Eve. While Rosa fed the child I gathered up what few belongings we needed to take with us and put them in a suitcase. I found a large plastic carrier bag to put the baby in. Then I had to leave and go to work. The day passed in a frenzy around me, while inside there was a stilled waiting. As usual, Penbridges gave each of us a small, wicker hamper packed with pieces of turkey, a bottle of wine, a pudding, and little jars of preserves, which I put to one side. This gesture, like all the others of the day, seemed at once endearing, and yet chilling, because this was a world I no longer inhabited. At five the store closed. We rushed to our lockers, changed out of our uniforms and then filed past the clock, which snapped our cards for a moment in its lips, registering our departure with a wheezing whir.

Rosa was sitting outside on the street, perched on the suitcase, the plastic bag sitting primly on her lap. I was suddenly very nervous. I took the bag from her and made my way back against the swell of the crowd. The store was in darkness but one of the managers was stretching up to shoot the last bolt on the door. I tapped on the glass. He peered out at me.

'What is it?' he cried.

'I've forgotten my hamper.'

He opened the door. I smiled at him, hoping that he would not look down into the bag. I could feel the baby stirring.

'You girls are all the same.' He sighed. 'Go on, then.'

Although the store was dark I knew its alleyways by heart. In the faint glow of light from the street I could make out the outline of the escalator. I climbed up its frozen steps to the first floor. There was no one about. I made straight for the crib, pushing aside the pew so I could get closer. I lifted the shiny plastic baby out, and from the bag gathered up Rosa's child and placed it in the hollowed-out manger. It was sleeping and barely stirred as I settled it. Rosa was right – in the darkness no one would know the difference. The pale faces of Joseph and Mary looked down lovingly at the dark creature. I put the doll in the bag. I found its glassy eyes and puckered, rosebud smile unsettling, so I covered it up. As I made my way down to the locker-room by a back stairway I thought for a moment about the child who would wake sometime in the night and wail, its cries echoing eerily around the empty store, which by then would be turning to coldness as the generators wound themselves down. I knew the pattern of the security men well. They would sit in their little box at the back entrance for the festive season, or go to a nearby pub and get quietly drunk. They would not hear the child, or if they did, would imagine it was some trick of the old building releasing the daytime cries of hundreds of children slowly into the night. When they dismantled the crib in the new year they would find a creature as dead and as frozen as the one originally placed there. And Rosa and I would be far away. From the deserted locker-room, its metal cabinets closed firmly

against me, I collected the hamper and put it in the bag. I
passed, unseen, by the staff entrance into a blind side-alley.

Rosa without her burden was almost gay. The Christmas lights strung across the scrawny neck of the street
blinked dazedly. Hoarse-voiced hawkers thrust great
bunches of balloons at us and frantic, whirring toys, furry
creatures with metal hearts embedded deep within them,
set off by the cold click of a key. We bought provisions –
freshly baked bread, bottles of stout, eggs, a side of ham
– because Father would have nothing in the house. From
a stall I bought a pair of gold earrings for Rosa. She put
them on immediately, catching her thin lobes between her
fingers as if each were a delicate scrap of gauze. We took
the train home, crushed up against one another, rocking
gently through the dark countryside, amid packages and
boxes and bright peals of laughter.

For once, Father seemed pleased to see us. We swept
through the house, cleaning and polishing. Rosa was
energetic at first, scrubbing away at encrusted stains on the
stove, but later she crumpled and I had to help her to
the sagging double bed we shared in the back room. For the
first time in years Father lit the Christmas candle and
left it burning in the dark hollow of the window while
we went to midnight mass together. The village church
was crowded. I was back once more in familiar territory,
among women with soft, sloping shoulders cowled in
downy coats. From the back it seemed they wore scarves
of children's arms, while other small hands clawed excit-

edly at the crooks of their elbows. Behind us there was
the scuffing of men and boys gathered at the back of the
church, and as always, that odour of candle grease which
as a child I thought was the smell of hair singeing in hell.

On Christmas morning Rosa and I moved the kitchen table
into the arms of the bay window and threw a white cloth
over it. The room was filled with bubbling smells as the
ham and pudding spluttered on the stove. Father sat in his
usual place by the fire, smiling moistly at us, as if sensing
that it would be our last time together. He never asked
about the child, although when we sat down to eat there
were stains on Rosa's blouse – her milk was coming in and
her swollen breasts were sore and tender. After dinner he
grew garrulous on the stout we had brought, and as we
cleared up, he began to sing in a voice entangled in phlegm:

There was an old woman and she lived in the woods
Weile, weile, wáile,
There was an old woman and she lived in the woods
Down by the river Sáile.

She had a baby three months old
Weile, weile, wáile,
She had a baby three months old
Down by the river Sáile.

She had a penknife long and sharp
Weile, weile, wáile,
She had a penknife long and sharp
Down by the river Sáile.

She stuck the penknife in the baby's heart
Weile, weile, wáile,
She stuck the penknife in the baby's heart
Down by the river Sáile . . .

From the scullery we joined in on the chorus, eyeing
one another as we carried him through verse after verse.
It made me wonder, as our voices rose and fell in ragged
unison, if we don't all have murder in our hearts.

A LAZY EYE

BELLA CARMICHAEL WOKE in a pool of blood. Startled, she lay rigid, afraid to move in case she would exacerbate the wound. She was surprised she felt no pain but the shock was probably acting as an anaesthetic. The sheet, blue in the moonlight, felt clammy around her loins. At first she thought it was the heat. It was a sticky night. Clouds raced across the moon in a thunderous flurry. The room juddered suddenly; the first breaking of the storm? Then it heaved again and she felt a rumbling beneath the floor. An earthquake. I have slept through the first great upheavals, she thought. The heaviness in my limbs is because I am pinned under some vast piece of fallen masonry. I should have stood under a door lintel, she thought. Only after several minutes when the wheels set up a clangour and there was a soft screech of brakes did she remember where she was. She was on a train, on the top bunk of a sleeper. Somewhere in Europe. Beneath her, a travelling companion who had boarded late the night before, groaned and turned over. Bella reached up and turned on the overhead light. There seemed to be blood everywhere – a huge stain beneath her, a clotted pattern on the top sheet, smears on her thighs. Damn it to hell, she cursed, my period.

Bella's trip had been dogged by small misfortunes and
large disappointments – waking on a bus journey having
dribbled on the lap of a nun, ousted by an attendant who
caught her washing her armpits in the ladies' room of a
motorway cafe, hissed at in the street by men in Naples.
There was the dismal business of tourist offices where
she had queued for hours, the crowded hostel rooms
with ragged underwear and socks hanging to dry on the
bed ends. It was not as she had expected. Setting out she
had envisaged being caught up in revolution, swept up
in some large-scale catastrophe, baton charges by police,
a bombing in a public place – only these things, she felt,
would give her stature. Instead here she was – in one of
the two Germanys, was it? – with no tampons.

Bella's preoccupation with other people's tragedies had
started years before with the death of President Kennedy.
She remembered the newspaper pictures of Caroline
Kennedy, a little freckled girl in a swing coat and ankle
socks, clutching her mother's hand at Arlington Cemetery.
Bella had been envious of her. She had been singled out,
given the chance to be heroic, the small solemnity of her
mourning emphasising the enormity of the offence. What
could Bella point to in her own life that was of such epic
proportion?

The Carmichaels went to school with their hems
hanging and sugar sandwiches in their satchels. They
slept two to a bed on sheets with a floral sprig pattern

that had long since faded into faint track marks as if some tiny insect had laboured across the snowy wastes of the material. They played on a green in front of the house, scorched in the summer, a mire in the winter. They ate their meals in relays because the kitchen wasn't big enough to accommodate them all at once. From the scullery there would be the hissing sound of frying, a plate of potato cakes would nosedive to the table and there would be a spasm of outstretched arms. There were *never* any leftovers in the Carmichael household. The hot press, wedged between the lavatory and the bathroom on the cramped landing, was a common store of smocked dresses, woollens – pale and shrunken – odd socks balled up like snail shells. You closed your eyes and fished something out; it became yours for the day. Meanwhile, Granny Carmichael dozed in the sunken settee in the living room among crumpled newspapers and flayed LPs out of their sleeves. Above her on the mantelpiece – since this was the good room – was a proud Manhattan of football trophies.

Bella searched in vain for some singularity in all of this. Her homely mother with the soft, embarrassed look of a woman who has just given birth – well, in fact, she usually had. There were eleven of them, after all. Her sister, Phyllis, was already a grandmother. All of them had been rudely healthy; none had succumbed to wasting diseases; the next generation was ruddy and bold. And who would have assassinated Bella's father?

He worked as a bank porter, standing to attention in a marbled lobby, his gold buttons gleaming, holding the door for customers. The only way he was likely to meet a violent, public death was at the hands of men in balaclavas with sawn-off shotguns. And even then, he was too comical and biddable a man to be killed thus. If a gang had held up the bank, Bella knew that he would have been the first to drop to the floor roaring 'Merciful hour!'

Bella had inherited her father's lazy eye. His gaze veered shiftily to the right as if something very lewd was going on behind other people's backs. As a child, Bella had thought of it as the evil eye, all-seeing, masterful. Until, that is, this congenital weakness of her father's emerged in her. Then it did not seem nearly dramatic enough. If it had been her choice Bella would have opted to be an albino like Deborah who lived two doors up – a short, white-headed girl with light, snowy lashes and pink, pained eyes. The other children regarded Deborah's short-sightedness as stupidity; they imitated her anguished grimace; they mimicked her dazed way of walking. But Bella saw her as saint-like, a precious, luminous creature, so sensitive that she could not bear the light of the world. She often speculated on how Deborah had come to be this way. Perhaps, at the moment of birth, a careless nurse had turned the full glare of the delivery room lamp on her and had scorched all the pigment from her skin and hair. Or, alternatively – an explanation which satisfied Bella more –

Deborah had witnessed something as a baby that had been
so frightful it had left her permanently pink with shame.
What was a lazy eye in comparison to that?

Nevertheless, for one glorious year, Bella too was
marked out. She had to wear a pair of glasses with the
right lens patched over with sticking plaster. It gave her
a lopsided, partial view of the world – a huge, pinkish
blur before her and a sensation of an obstruction looming
ahead which was never encountered but yet never went
away. She sometimes feared that this flesh-coloured wall
that met her gaze was, in fact, a fresh layer of skin growing
over the unused eye. Frequently she had to take the glasses
off to reassure herself that her walled-up eye was still there,
and still worked.

'Is it sore?' her schoolfriends asked about the eclipsed
eye, associating sticking plaster with pain. Some were
convinced that Bella did not have a second eye; others
that she had been badly scarred and it was too unsightly
to expose. Her good eye languishing in its pink prison
elicited a mixture of pity and regret. Bella was exempted
from rough games; in the playground she was allowed to
stand in at skipping in case a crack of the rope might send
her glasses flying. Behind her back she knew they called
her specky two-eyes but it was better than being 'just one
of those Carmichaels'.

Even among the Carmichaels, Bella's spectacles were
treated with a solicitude that was rarely shown to her.
'Where are Bella's glasses?' her mother would demand

before each mealtime sitting as if they had a life independent of their owner. And Granny Carmichael was never allowed to reverse into the sofa or a fireside chair before the cushions were first checked for Bella's specs. Bella had always been a poor reader, besieged at school by hissing prompters as the gap between each of her blurted-out words yawned. But that year she was never once asked to read aloud. She discovered that the glasses with the patch were a protection behind which she could lazily daydream. And, in time, she grew to regard the unexposed part of her face as something magical, an obvious but secret wound, an area of deep mystery unclaimed by the world. And when the plaster was eventually removed the skin around her right eye had a pale, sickly look like the papery relic of a saint. Alas, the treatment worked. The lazy eye had righted itself and within six months, Bella didn't even have to wear glasses anymore.

Dawn crept into the compartment. Bella eased the blind up and watched as the night disappeared in long streaks of indigo cloud and a weak sun rose in the huge, bleached, watery sky. The train shuttled past dark, wooden-framed farmhouses huddled together like beasts averting their eyes from something ancient and frightening. Bella hung over the edge of her bunk and watched as the countryside passed like a speckled scarf drawn over her features – a toss of angry trees in her hair, the steep rise of pasture on her cheeks, a pair of boulders for her eyes. Fleeing through the early morning the train made hardly an impression on the landscape; it could not even boast of a shadow, Bella thought. She roused herself from her vacant-eyed stupor. What was she going to do about the mess in the bed? Her predicament reminded her of Franny, her next sister up, with whom she had shared a bed through her girlhood. Franny had been a bed-wetter. She slept so heavily that she never woke in time to make it to the toilet. She was a fat, indolent girl and the family considered this just another manifestation of her laziness. Bella would wake to the stench of pee and a sensation of hot seepage around her arse and Franny sitting on the side of the bed, head hanging, shoulders hunched, shivering and, Bella realised now, ashamed. But then she was convinced that Franny did it on purpose. And once her nocturnal crime was committed, Franny seemed incapable of remedying it. It was Bella who would have to get up and strip the bed while Franny stood listlessly to one side clutching her soaked nightie. Afterwards they would climb back into bed silently, carefully avoiding the damp spot in the middle covered now by the top sheet, and pulling the blankets up to their chins, they would turn away from one another resolutely and sleep back to back. In the morning, though, when Mrs Carmichael came to rouse them, it was Bella who would call out – 'Franny's done it again!'

Bella eased herself out of the sodden bunk and down the

stepladder. Throwing on her dressing-gown she slipped
into the deserted passageway and fled to the lavatory at
the end of the carriage. If, at that moment, she could have
leapt from the train without injuring herself, she would
have done it. When she returned, the mystery occupant of
the lower bunk was brushing her teeth at the tiny basin in
the compartment. She was a large-boned young woman of
about Bella's own age, with a fringe of heavy fair hair and a
scrubbed complexion. She wore oversized, white pyjamas
with navy piping on the collar. She stopped brushing as
Bella came in. She had a rather fierce air, stooped thus,
her teeth bared and little gobbets of toothpaste foaming
at the corners of her mouth.

'Hello,' Bella said cautiously.

The girl nodded amiably. She spat noisily into the basin
and wiped her mouth with a towel. Then she uncapped
a bottle of breath freshener and with the exuberance of a
schnapps drinker she tossed it back and gargled noisily,
her throat rippling, her eyes rolling in the back of her
head. Bella waited. She might as well have been in the back
bedroom with Franny; travel might broaden the mind but
it forced the body into the most narrow confines of intimacy with strangers. A jet of peppermint-coloured liquid
was spewed into the basin, the tap was turned on to wash
it away and then the girl turned and extended a hand.

'How do you do?'

She said this with the careful enunciation of one
tackling a second language.

'My name is Irma. Good morning!'

Bella smiled tightly, her mind racing. She did not want to get trapped into pleasantries knowing what she had to ask this woman and the longer the pleasantries persisted the harder it would be to broach the subject.

'May I ask you something?'

'Ja! Sure!' Irma nodded enthusiastically.

'You wouldn't have any . . . tampons?' She said the last word with emphasis.

Irma knitted her brow.

'Sanitary towels?' Bella ventured.

'Ah, towel!' Irma plucked from the basin the towel she had been using and proffered it.

'No, no . . . sanitary pads.'

Irma shook her head quizzically.

'Period,' Bella said pointing extravagantly to herself. 'Blood.'

'Blood?' Irma looked alarmed.

If she didn't make herself clear soon, this girl would think she was a nutcase, Bella thought. She reached up and grabbed a fistful of bloody sheet from her bed.

'Ah, ja!' Irma smiled broadly. 'It's Auntie Jane, ja?'

Bella's father had financed her trip. Enda Carmichael, door-opener. He had left money. Not much, but they had all been surprised that he had any at all. Bella imagined him picking up and saving every dropped coin in the bank for forty years and putting them by. For what? For her, it had

49

turned out. For Bella, my youngest daughter, the proceeds of my savings account. She was, along with her mother, the only one to be named. She wondered why. Granted, she had seen him through his final months – she was the only one of the brood now at home. Maybe her name was the only one of the eleven that came to mind. (He often got the girls mixed up. Their names were tradeable.) Or perhaps he had intended it this way all along? While she had longed for a father other than him, and a glamorous, dead version at that, he had been, in his way, singling her out for special attention.

Had Bella Carmichael and Irma Kalinin become friends they might, in years to come, have laughed about that early morning introduction, exaggerating the gulf of misunderstanding between them with each retelling. As it was, they smiled shyly about it over breakfast in the dining car and engaged in the small talk of low-budget travellers. That hostel in Vienna – eyes turned heavenward. How their paths had crossed unknowingly in Berlin. There was a beer hall in Munich Bella simply had to see; a cathedral in Budapest Irma mustn't miss. It struck Bella that at any given time Europe was being traversed by thousands of people plodding dutifully after one another on a sort of dull crusade, following the same route and using the same guidebook. It certainly convinced her that independent travel was neither spontaneous nor anonymous. Rather, she had felt like a piece of luggage abandoned on an airport carousel, going endlessly round and round. And as for anonymity, there was a letter from her mother at each *poste restante*. Of course, she needn't have collected any of them but it made her feel anchored in a new city to know that somewhere in a pigeon-hole in a gloomy post office a letter lay with her name on it. Through these letters the Carmichaels travelled with her. Across the seas the primacy of *their* news echoed – Johnny's new apprentice, Peggy's wedding plans, little Ivor's first words. This plaintive incantation of domestic news seemed more concrete than any of Bella's own experiences. If she had written back she would have been reduced to describing the grandeur of Rome. And what would they have made of that?

As Bella and Irma made their way back to their compartment, the train attendant who usually sat in a little cabin at the end of the carriage brushed past them. He was a small man with large brown eyes and a curiously aristocratic-looking moustache. There were nicotine stains on his fingers. He had appeared after they had crossed the Polish frontier, replacing the large Russian woman who wore a tight black pencil skirt and her blonded hair up. She would gratuitously lock the door of the toilet between stations and retreat to her little den where, Bella suspected, she grappled with passengers in a crumb-ridden bed or napped fully-clothed. She responded to any entreaty with a stony 'Niet!' This man, in comparison, had seemed almost pleadingly friendly. He always left the door of the cabin open. From outside it looked warm and dishevelled like an animal's lair. He kept the blind drawn so the light inside was brown and mottled. He brewed tea on a stove in the corner and made sandwiches with large beef tomatoes which he kept in a muslin bag under his bunk.

Now he strode purposefully by them, looking cross. He had been busy in their absence. There were great mounds of bed linen all along the corridors; he had stripped the beds. Bella was relieved. They were about to enter their compartment when he came up behind them again. He was accompanied by a ticket collector, a tall, stern-looking man with a pocked face and large hands, a bulky book of timetables tucked under his arm. The attendant pointed at Bella and expostulated in a rush of French.

'What's he saying?' Bella asked Irma.

'He is asking is this your compartment,' Irma repeated after the attendant. Bella nodded.

The attendant stooped and lifted one of her sheets from the floor. In the full glare of morning, the blood-stains looked deliberate, sinister. There was another rush of words from the attendant – agitation turning to anger.

'He asks what has been going on here,' Irma intoned.

Several passengers, hearing the commotion, came to the doors of their compartments. The attendant pointed to the sheet again and spat out another sentence.

'Animals. You are animals. What is going on here? Animals.' Out of Irma's cool mouth the words seemed disconnected like a soundtrack out of synch with the film.

The attendant poked a finger at Bella's breast.

'He is saying you should be ashamed of yourself.' Irma persisted dutifully with the translation. '*Never* in all his life has he . . . '

He peered around the door of the compartment. His eyes narrowed. Some new accusation was about to be levelled. Bella held her breath.

'What perversions have you indulged in?' Bella felt she was now being directly accused by Irma. 'There has been evil-doing here.'

Irma delivered this with an air of finality. For the first time she met Bella's eye.

'Tell him,' Bella pleaded, 'for God's sake, tell him.'

'Elle a ses regles,' Irma said.

'Tell him I will pay for the sheets. How much? How much?'

'Elle a ses regles,' Irma repeated. 'Mon amie paiera.'

The attendant shouted back, spittle on his lips, and pointed to the ticket collector.

'They do not want your money,' Irma said regretfully. 'They want you to leave the train.'

It was somewhere in Belgium; that was all she knew. A small town; a two-minute stop. The ticket collector, on whose authority she had been banished, helped her with her bags. The other passengers crowded into the gangway, murmuring quietly to one another. There was a shocked, subdued atmosphere as in the moments after news of a great tragedy has been received. They stood back to let her by, recoiling as she passed in case they might be contaminated. She wondered if afterwards they would fall upon the bloodied sheets and tear them into pieces for souvenirs. Irma was nowhere to be seen, skulking in the compartment, no doubt. Bella did not know what she had expected of her. Some outrage, perhaps.

'Don't they understand?' she had asked Irma. 'I didn't do it on purpose, it just happened. I wasn't expecting it. Don't they know that women bleed?'

Irma shrugged and stuffed a pair of shoes into Bella's bag. She helped Bella pack with the same glassy indifference with which she had translated the attendant's French. Perhaps she, too, thought there was something unnatural about it, though quite what Bella couldn't figure out. What was she being accused of?

She stepped off the train. It was a glorious day, a blue sky woolly with cloud. The sun felt warm on her cheeks or perhaps she was just flushed. The ticket collector slung her last bag out after her. It landed in a heap at her feet; this, she felt, was what he wished to do with *her*. She sensed the gaze of many eyes upon her as the door wheezed shut and the train lurched once before slowly chugging away. She stared defiantly after it; she was determined to be dignified. She had, after all, been waiting for this moment all of her life.

She waited until the train was out of sight before sitting dejectedly on her bags. She sighed and looked around her at the uncaring landscape, flat and treeless. Across the tracks stood a small stone station house. The rails hummed in the heat. She felt curiously deflated. She had expected there to be more exhilaration. Instead, she felt merely punished.

It was no different from all the other reversals on her travels – and in her life before that. She thought about home – the ramshackle house on Vandeleur Green, the crowded bedrooms, the lack of privacy and space, the pans of white bread and the cheap cuts of meat. The sum of all these small humiliations, *these* were what had marked her out. There would be no large, singular event to validate her existence. There would only be more of this – official retribution for bleeding in public. She felt as she did when the doctor had first taken the glasses with the eye patch off; her vision unobscured, her lazy eye finally cured.

THE CANTILEVER
PRINCIPLE

'TRUSSED-UP', my father was saying, 'like a chicken. Oven-ready!' He beamed at me, grateful for my indulgence – I had heard the story several times over – then turned back to Sam.

'They daubed this stuff on me, like washing-up liquid. Rubbed it on neat – all over!'

'By the prettiest nurse, no doubt, Jack!' Uncle Sam winked extravagantly.

They were like boys again, gleeful with reprieve. Sam, snowy-haired, with a grizzled jaw, and my father, propped up on the pillows, his face ripe and waxy as a windfallen apple. The danger had passed. We were safely allowed our gaiety. Indeed, it was necessary because we had so nearly lost him. We lost my mother – early. For years he had measured time by her death. That was, he would say, puckering his brow, that was just before we lost your mother. That was his word for it. Lost.

I cannot remember her now except as a collection of sensations cut adrift – the smell of cold cream, the steady thump of another heart, a benign shape leaning over me as a prelude to embrace. He was generous with details of her. They had met at a tea dance at the Metropole. She was a good deal younger than him. He had been accused of cradle-snatching. They had walked out together for eight months. Her family did not approve. After they were married his landlady let her move in. Then there was the flat by the canal before they bought a home – here. This other world that they belonged to, grey and grainy, the one before I was born, this was where I was convinced my mother was lost. I identified the year as 1947, the worst winter on record, and pictured her wandering in a blizzard in the wrap-around coat and angora beret she wore in those long-ago holiday snaps. These seemed always to be taken in winter, at the edge of cliffs, my mother's hair wild around her face, her teeth chattering with cold through a brave smile. My father, it has to be said, looks pretty goofy in these pictures. The short-back-and-sides haircut, his large ears, a gormless sort of smile. He has improved with age. Whereas she seems perfect then, for then, as if she somehow knew . . . but, no, that's ascribing premonition to mere candour for the camera.

Of her death he would not speak. A brain haemorrhage. My only guide is Mrs Parfitt. He had left for work. And where was I? Somewhere out of the picture. My mother is sitting over the debris of breakfast things. It is a wan April morning aching to be spring. She is gazing out the kitchen window, elbows propped on the table, one hand clasping a cup of luke-warm tea. Suddenly there is an intruder who strikes her one blow on the temple sending everything

spinning. The cup leaps from her hand, a plate slides off
the edge of the table. She tries to rise but her arm buckles
beneath her, crumpling the waxed folds of the oiled cloth
and rattling the teapot. Her last view is of the mocking
darkness of its spout. My father finds her at lunchtime, face
bathed in milk, crumbs in her hair, dried blood around her
ear. He thinks she has passed out or, comically, has fallen
asleep. He leaves her be and calls a neighbour – the inner
workings of women are no business of his. *She* knows.

'She's dead, Mr Eustace,' Mrs Parfitt says, 'your wife
is dead.' Here, she says, here at this very table.

Without a mother, not only death, but birth, too, was
a mystery. We found you in a basket on the canal,
my father used to say. I liked the 'we' in this; for
the first time it included me. And it beat those stories
about cabbage leaves. I could imagine this. The pair of
them walking along the towpath near the gasworks and
finding a Moses basket in the green, scummy water by
the bank. My mother (wearing the same hat and coat;
there are no costume changes for her) lifts me out carefully.

'Ah look,' she says, 'look at the wee mite.'

I am wearing a long white christening robe.

'John, just look.'

She hoists me up on her shoulder and turns around
so that he is looking directly into my eyes. Was it then
it started – this fierce, reluctant attachment?

She swings around, her voice brimming with excitement and says: 'Shall we keep her?' as if it's the most reckless, daring adventure they have ever considered.

My father says yes.

Hospital time is different. Elongated. It was – is – high summer but already the recent gusty, blue-bright days and cool, lilac evenings belong to a carefully delineated past. Even the heartbreaking sunsets, melancholy and grand, which accompanied my vigil, now seem like the fevered reproduction of some long distant memory. A by-pass. Appropriate surgery for the man. My father, the engineer. Bridges were his thing. During school holidays we made pilgrimages to them. I remember a misty January evening standing reverentially by the Forth Bridge which rose like a giant brontosaurus out of the still waters.

'The cantilever principle,' my father said importantly. 'See, the three spans.' He pointed, one hand on my shoulder. 'They each stand separately but when projected towards each other they form a bridge. Stress against stress.'

I was terrified that he would die.

'Don't worry,' Sam had said, 'he's a hardy one.' But the warning signs, once glimpsed, will never go away. His breathlessness, the alarming puce of his cheeks, the panic in his eye. I had seen them all and knew the cold, hard dread they induced in me. I grew to hate him for his frailty. I despised him when he gasped for air. I turned away, ashamed, when he clutched his chest in pain. I told myself he was pretending, doing it for effect, and that sympathy would only make him weaker. He had deceived me. His robust good health all these years had been a sham. He had secretly been cultivating the germ of his own death.

Intensive Care. My father adrift somewhere while all around him gadgets did his struggling for him. There was a bleeping green monitor and the noisy shuffling of a ventilator. Narrow tubes snaked in under the bedclothes and a bulbous bag of intravenous drip stood sentry at the bedhead. It reminded me of the pictures of bridges he collected, all huge beams and girders and in between the steel and metal latticework, a tiny train trapped.

The hardware hid him from me; all his fear and helplessness put on hold.

'It's quite normal,' one of the nurses assured me, 'we keep them heavily sedated. Lessens the likelihood of rejection.'

For days I sat by his bedside or paced up and down the phlegm-coloured corridors. The light there was dull and dead as if it, too, had been etherised. And the noise – like the muted clamour of a penitentiary. The wheeling and droning of cleaners, the rattle of trolleys shivering with instruments, the clangour of bed pans, gave way to periods of forsaken quiet. At night, after visiting hour, it seemed as if we were on board a ghostly liner, abandoned and adrift. Sometimes I would go to the Day Room. A television with the sound turned down was perched high on a ledge. Animated faces on the screen mouthed messages to the silent room. Several patients would be slumped in the leatherette armchairs which broke wind when they sat down. Their slippers chafed the shiny lino. Some of them had crude crosses in gentian violet daubed on their faces to mark where they'd been treated. It was also a cancer hospital.

That must have been what he had. My friend. That's what I thought of him as, although we never spoke. He was in the ward opposite the intensive care unit, his bed just inside the door. He was a young man, the same age as me, perhaps. He lay on the bed in pyjama bottoms and a dressing gown, open and stranded around his waist. There was, to look at him, no sign of illness except for the shaved rectangle at his temple. Beneath the hurtful ridge of his brow his eyes were sunken, fogged-looking, slow to register, and yet, I had the feeling that I was being watched intensely. He was stricken on one side. Above his head like a noose, a tubular triangle hung. With one arm he used this to manoeuvre himself in the bed. He moved his good leg constantly, grinding his heel against the bedclothes like the restless kicking of a baby. Everything about him was like a baby. The awful trustfulness of his gaze. The little identity tag around his wrist with those bare details with which he had come into the world – his name, his date of birth. He seemed utterly defenceless and alone.

And yet, he was not alone. A woman, Miriam, (I gave her a name, but never him) came daily, kissing him on the forehead before settling down in a chair beside his bed. She moved with what seemed like exaggerated care as if any sudden gesture might startle him. He watched her silently, following her about wonderingly with his eyes. He would grasp her hand, rubbing his fingers on her knuckles as if touch were new to him. I could hear her speak soothingly to him.

Intimacy is shocking in a hospital, absurd amidst the starch and clatter, and *their* tenderness, especially, seemed alien. But I couldn't take my eyes off them. She drew things from a crowded tote bag like a conjurer desperate to please. She brought flowers which she carefully arranged in a jug beside the bed. Once she sellotaped a child's drawing to the side of his locker. She fed him, handing him a cup with a straw in it to drink from. She wiped his mouth. She peeled fruit for him – oranges, bananas – holding them up in front of him before clamping his fingers firmly around them. It was like watching a mother and child. I felt as I do when women breastfeed in public. The fear of other people's nakedness.

I never wanted to know any more about him except what I could learn from watching. Perhaps I knew the bargain I was about to make. His life for one I valued more.

'And at last Pharaoh made a proclamation to the whole

of his people: Whenever a male child is born, cast it into the river, keep only the girls alive. And now one of the descendants of Levi wooed and married a woman of his own clan, who conceived and bore him a son. So winning were the child's looks that for three months she kept him hidden away; then, unable to conceal him any longer, she took a little basket of reeds, which she smeared with clay and pitch, and in this put her baby son down among the bulrushes on the river bank . . . '

On the third day there was a change in my father's condition. I detected this only by a certain change in the atmosphere, an added grim bustle in the room. The nurses, usually chatty and given to small talk, instead conferred with one another at the door casting anxious glances in my direction. They made what seemed to be futile adjustments to the equipment, picked up my father's lumpen hand to get a pulse with an air of resignation, leafed through his charts as if searching for some clue to his condition they'd overlooked. I didn't ask them, of course, what they thought was wrong. I was too afraid. 'Not responding,' was a phrase I overheard.

Meanwhile in the ward opposite, my friend was celebrating. He was in a wheelchair by the bed, a rug thrown over his legs. Above him, hanging from the curtain rails was an array of balloons and streamers, and Miriam was stringing together a loop of cards behind his bed. It was his birthday. In the afternoon visiting hour, a gang of people arrived. They drew up in a circle around him. Some perched on the bed, others stood. There was the popping of corks and a rush of paper cups to catch the foaming champagne. There were bursts of raucous laughter, an air of triumph.

'Come on,' someone called out to one of the nurses, 'join the party!'

'Ye'll all be thrown out,' she warned mockingly.

A loud 'awh' from the group.

I couldn't see him in the midst of them but I imagined him there smiling jaggedly, drunk with memory. When the visitors' bell rang at four they wheeled him recklessly out of the ward and down the corridor towards the Day Room, whooping and singing – 'Happy birthday to you, happy birthday to you, happy birthday dear . . . ' The swing doors closed behind them.

Three a.m. Condition, stable. They had told me to go home but I wouldn't. I didn't trust them. I was a nuisance, I knew that, prowling around, nervously alert from lack of sleep and haunted by unspoken fears. Even Sam had got irritated.

'Don't do the martyr on us. For God's sake, go home. There's nothing you can do here,' he had said when he left at midnight. He was right; there was nothing I could do – there or anywhere else. But I thought that any sudden movement of mine might precipitate disaster. As long as I was there, nothing could happen to him.

There is something sacred about those early hours of the morning. A hush. It isn't difficult to see why death comes then, how it gains easeful entry when the defences of the world are down. The graveyard hours. If Dad makes it through these, I thought, he will make it through another day. It was then I remembered my friend. I slipped out of Intensive Care and crossed the corridor. He too was sleeping. It was a warm night and he had thrown off all the bedclothes except for a sheet swaddled around his groin. In the blue light his limbs looked startlingly beautiful; there were perfect half-moons on all his fingernails.

A breeze sighed softly at the open window. I thought of wind among rushes. It would be easy now to push him forth out into the calm waters of the night in this, the easeful hour. I laid my hand on his pillow. There would be no struggle. In his slumber he would barely notice the gentle rocking of the basket. He was the boy-child, the one who must be sacrificed. And, in return, my father would be saved. Take him, I urged the darkness, take *him*.

By the next morning my father was awake, in a different ward, the hardware all removed. He smiled sheepishly at me as I came in, as if he'd been away on a drunken binge.

'I'm sorry,' he said weakly, 'for giving you a fright.'

'You had us worried, you old dog,' Sam said, 'we'd thought you'd given up the ghost. Isn't that right, Kate?'

For days, almost a week, I dared not see my friend. It was easy to avoid him. His ward was on the floor below and I did not have to pass it now. Only when my father could leave his bed did I have the courage to venture down. I walked along the familiar corridor, halting at his doorway. The bed was empty, the locker cleared. The child's drawing had been torn roughly from its spot leaving only a corner scrap. The coverlet on the bed did not even bear the outline of his body.

'Gone, my dear,' a nurse said as she bustled past.

I did not – could not – ask what she meant by gone.

I watch out for him on the street now. Certain men remind me of him. I see them in pubs, on trains, in buses, and my heart leaps. I am about to rush up to them when they turn around and reveal themselves as imposters. Anyway, I know it's all in vain. I know the price that's been exacted. I *know* that I will never see him again.

THE PLAYHOUSE

'WHY DON'T YOU show Helen the playhouse?' Sue's voice called from the kitchen.

Outside on an apron of hot concrete a woman and a barefoot child stood. Lucy dutifully took Helen's hand and led her round the corner of the house which cast a shadow over half of the garden. She led Helen along the dark promontory of the chimney's shade which extended furthest into the bright sunlight. The garden was dishevelled-looking and neglected in places. Weeds sprouted up through the crazy-paving path, convolvulus slyly trumpeted in the greenery. They passed a failed vegetable patch. As they emerged from the shadow Sue came to the kitchen window, another child slung on her hip, a damp tea-towel bunched in her hand. She watched as they picked their way slowly across the littered lawn, hand-in-hand like playmates. Her daughter, a sturdy, solemn six-year-old whose hair at the temples had been bleached almost white by the sun that summer, and her friend, gracefully boyish, slender, long-necked, her cropped, flaxen hair bound up in a bandeau, her pale, floral dress showing a damp, creased patch at the back from where she had been sitting. Sue, smiling, turned back into the dim interior.

They climbed a bank at the end of the garden on which the playhouse stood. Lucy crouched and went in and Helen, carefully tucking her dress under her, crawled in after. The house was shadowy and cool. It smelled of moss and rotting wood. In the dappled light Helen's arms looked bruised.

'Is this where you play, Lucy?' she asked lamely.

The child was busily dragging a cardboard box into the centre of the floor. She hauled out a tea-set.

'I bring my friends here.'

'Am I your friend then?' Helen bit her lip. Fishing for compliments from a six-year-old was less than dignified.

'Would you like some tea?'

'Mmn,' said Helen as enthusiastically as she could. She dreaded games, expecting all the time to be found out as being less than whole-hearted in her pretence. Lucy laid out several red and yellow plastic cups and made hissing sounds to indicate that tea was being made. Helen, embarrassed, looked away.

'I'll be in town shopping on Saturday. Why don't I pick you up at the supermarket?' Sue had said.

The forecourt of a shopping centre seemed a strangely neutral place for friends to meet, more suited to blackmailers or illicit lovers, Helen thought as she waited. She watched as Sue struggled across the car park with the children. She was a big-boned, generous woman with a mass of ginger hair, a freckled face, a broad, eager smile and strong, shapely arms – she had once been a swimming champion. Helen trooped behind the trolley as the pile of groceries mounted behind child number two. She chided herself for referring to Sue's children in serial numbers and then marvelled at the agility of the mental adjustment – this was actually Sue's third child.

'John Andrew, terrible handle, isn't it?' Sue grimaced. 'The Andrew bit was my idea. Wasn't going to let the old bag have all her own way.'

The old bag was Frank's mother.

'And no one's going to shorten it, isn't that right, chickpea?'

She chucked the child under the chin. These were Sue's victories.

'Could you be a love, Helen, and get the washing-up liquid?'

Helen headed for Detergents. Such errands rendered her a nervous child again. She dithered, unable to make a choice. The lemon-scented one or the one for softer hands? Or the cheap green-coloured one? Her occasional visits to Sue were marked by such calculations. She always dressed down out of a consideration she guessed to be smug, knowing she could not bear Sue's pitiful envy as she fingered the stuff of one of Helen's shop-bought dresses. On this occasion Lucy came to the rescue, rounding the corner under a large packet of disposable nappies.

'The green one,' she said simply.

'You can sleep in Lucy's room, she'll bunk in with John Andrew,' Sue said as they went upstairs.

Helen, following her, noticed that she had got heavier; she had the burly authority now of a *hausfrau*, and with it a kind of easy capability which Helen envied. Sue turned down the coverlet on the bed, an oddly touching maternal gesture. It was a typical little girl's room. A row of ragdolls and teddy bears sat on a toy chest in one corner, there was a Brer Rabbit table lamp, colouring books by the bedside, alphabet wallpaper. Later, lying on the bedsheets which bore the milky smell of a child, Helen would hear Frank and Sue moving about in the next room. She would plug her ears with cotton wool for fear of eavesdropping on the sounds of love. Sue would have scoffed at that had she known. Gone past all of that now, she would have said, small kids really knock it out of you. Too tired to think at the end of the day, let alone . . .

Helen stood for several minutes, the ragdolls regarding her dolefully – the interloper. She abandoned her bag and went downstairs. Sue was chopping onions.

'Can I help?' she asked.

'No, no,' Sue said, 'you go on outside. Relax, relax, you're the visitor . . . '

Helen and Sue. Born in the same calendar month. Friends from childhood. Their initials, intertwined, carved on a desk somewhere. Listless hours shared in bedrooms listening to records and feeding infatuations. Tennis hops. The lonely vigour of gropings with boys. Discoveries. Helen was adopted; Sue's first pregnancy, Lucy – unplanned. There were mannerisms of Sue's that Helen considered proprietorially as hers, so familiar were they. How she would whistle through her teeth when impressed by something; the way she would swat her fringe away from her face. And there were other things. Her crooked index finger broken in the swimming baths and set badly. Her favourite colour – cerise – her blood type, B positive. There was a time when they knew one another's waist measurements. The last time she had visited they had sunbathed and Helen had noticed with a gentle shock the scar on Sue's abdomen from John Andrew's birth – a Caesarean. She felt, ridiculously, that she should have been informed.

The front door slammed.

'Hello?'

'Frank,' Sue said as if explanation were necessary.

'Ah, Helen, welcome,' he said coming into the room and shaking her hand manfully. He had recently had his hair cut which gave him the scrubbed, wasted look of a convict. He was an uneasy man, with small, watchful eyes. He winced when he greeted people as if they had sent electric currents through his fingers.

'How's the work?'

'Fine, fine.'

'And the flat? Get all that legal stuff sorted out?'

'Yes, yes, the solicitor you recommended was very helpful.'

Helen found conversations with Frank rather like job interviews.

'Good, good.' He nodded, taking off his jacket and loosening his tie.

'Dinner ready?'

Sue came to the table bearing a large casserole dish. He wrapped an arm around her waist.

'How's the little woman?'

'Careful, hot!' she warned moving deftly out of his grasp. Frank smiled at Helen in his pained way.

'Have you washed your hands, Luce?' Sue demanded.

Lucy clambered down and headed towards the sink. Sue sank into a chair.

'Something to drink?' Frank asked.

'Wine in the fridge,' Sue said wearily. 'Helen brought it.'

'You girls have a great life, drinking in the afternoon, no less!'

'We didn't . . . ' Sue began but John Andrew, seated belligerently in his high chair, set up a wail.

'Here, let Mummy cut that up for you.'

Sue leaned across and chopped up the meat in his dish. From the sink a great cloud of steam rose up. Lucy yelped.

'Ooh, I've burned myself . . . the water's too hot.'

Sue shot up almost colliding with Frank who was brandishing the bottle of wine as if it were material evidence.

'Fancy label, eh?' he said. 'None of your cheap plonk!'

He poured a glass for Helen. At the sink Lucy was dancing with pain, her scalded hand between her thighs. Sue was trying to apply salve.

'Can I do anything?' Helen appealed to no one in particular.

Frank touched her gently on the forearm.

'Take no notice,' he said, 'all in a day's work.'

'This is just like old times,' Sue said as they sat over the dinner-table. The room was bathed in a bleached, pink twilight. The empty wine bottle, like a patient hourglass, stood among the debris. From the next room, sounds of grief came from an unwatched television. Overhead, bed-time was in progress. Helen could hear Lucy scampering from room to room, squealing, with Frank tramping heavily behind her making growling sounds.

'He's like another child,' Sue said, shaking her head.

They fell silent.

'And how have *you* been?' Helen asked tentatively. 'Really?'

She added the last word as a sort of shorthand to indicate seriousness, adult talk.

'Oh,' said Sue, rubbing her temple. 'Tired. Never time to draw a breath.'

She smiled wanly.

'That's not what I meant.'

'You mean Kevin, I suppose.'

The name had been uttered. The dead child. The second one between Lucy and John Andrew. Drowned. The irony of it, Helen thought. Drowned in a swimming pool. With Sue watching. Or rather, with Sue not watching.

'I only looked away for a minute,' she would reiterate in the days following the funeral.

'I had just taken his water wings off . . . ' she would continue, lapsing into a mechanical but entranced re-counting of the event which Helen grew to know so well. One minute he was splashing about on the steps, the next he was a pale, fleshy blur on the pool's peppermint floor. Peppermint. That word, that absurd detail always struck Helen as somehow sinister. Peppermint. He just slipped away, Sue would say. To Helen it sounded rather soothing, like a swan gliding off. She had expected terror, a great thrashing about, a gasping for air. Something, Sue would say, something caught my attention, I don't know what. A flash of colour? Did someone wave or call my name? Some commotion at the deep end? Frank says it was God distracting me so I wouldn't see him being taken. Rubbish, Helen had said, and then felt immediately remorseful because it might have provided Sue with some kind of comfort. Sue had ruminated for several weeks over what had caused her momentary inattention, what could have been so important then and so trivial now that she could not remember it. It tormented her, this missing clue, as if it alone could explain why Kevin had died. And then she stopped wondering, aloud at any rate, and after a few months she ceased talking about it altogether.

Wasn't it lucky she was pregnant, people had whispered to one another at the graveside, eyeing Sue's bump warily. And that it's safe. By this they meant that wasn't it lucky that the shock had not induced premature labour but it came out quite differently, to Helen at least. To her it sounded as if the new baby were some malevolent usurper claiming his right to the throne. The life counter in the equation with death. And the preoccupation with safety made Sue out to be some kind of monster whose children must be protected from her. Helen thought of the baby within, gurgling in a cushion of flesh and fluid, the safest place it could be and not so far removed from the warm, watery world that Kevin had been spirited away to. A water baby, Sue had called him. A water baby.

'It's been almost two years now, Helen.'

Helen felt reproved, the child shut out. There seemed huge impossibilities in their conversations now, areas that could not be ventured into safely. Helen could not remember if it was marriage or the lost child that had created the gap.

'Frank's been really good,' Sue said finally, 'I couldn't have managed without him.'

It was not always so, Helen thought spitefully. Sue rose and started stacking the plates.

'Better get this mess cleared up.'

She padded towards the sink.

'It's so lovely to see you,' she called over her shoulder. 'We really should keep up with one another more. Locked up with the kids all day turns you into a moron. I long sometimes for a grown-up conversation, know what I mean?' She laughed a shade too brightly. 'I depend on you, Helen, for news of the outside world, the *real* world.'

Helen looked out into the garden strewn with abandoned playthings – a keeled-over bicycle, an upturned buggy, a skipping rope, several dolls, one naked, another armless like the victims of some mindless massacre. They held for Helen a cruel, embracing logic.

'But isn't this the real world for you?' she asked gesturing to the darkening garden.

'Oh no,' Sue said drawing the curtains swiftly as if Helen had gazed too long at something intimate. 'No, we're just playing. Playing house.'

IN TIMES
OF WAR

ANOTHER WOMAN HAS entered my home. Against my will, though I suppose it could be said I let her in. Not wittingly, of course. But one evening when I opened the door to Michael I knew that she was there, standing with him in the shadows. And when my back was turned she slipped in by me and took up residence. I wondered why she had lodged with me, her natural enemy. You would imagine she would be uncomfortable here in occupied territory, behind the lines, alone and friendless. But she's learned the tricks of stealth and travelling undercover. No one on the street has the slightest idea there is a stranger in my house. She comes and goes undetected. Her papers are in order, I suppose. Who'd question *her* right to exist? Certainly not the authorities . . , in times of war, we trade on our legitimacy.

Michael's in the army. It's how we met – at one of those large parties we used to have early on to celebrate. A victory, I suppose. In the days when we counted them. Now we haven't got the energy. It was in a large ballroom in the bombed-out part of the city which then seemed only temporary. In fact people used to go there sightseeing – before they got used to living among ruins. There were

streamers and balloons, I remember, a dance band and a
jovial master of ceremonies sporting a dickie bow. He told
war jokes; you know, Tommies and Krauts. At that stage
none of us took it seriously. Of course it wasn't *this* war
he was talking about.

I associate Michael with the mood of that night – the
loud triumph of brass and the headlong rush towards danger. We danced – badly. Funny, I expected the opposite. I
thought that along with all those parade drills they'd teach
the officers to dance, a necessary social skill like caning
privates. But no, that isn't fair. We are at war, after all.

I didn't like peace-time. It didn't allow me to live as
I live now. I wouldn't have met Michael, for one. But
it isn't just that. At first, you see, the war paralysed me.
My life seemed small, unimportant, all my preoccupations
ridiculous. I watched TV for days in a kind of stupor
feeling in some strange way that it was my duty, that the
least I could do was to be informed. Except, of course,
that we got so little information, or we got the same
information repeated, time and time again. And then, it
was so far away – a distant city in a desert. The infidels,
the infidels, they warned us. But, to tell the truth, there
was a feeling of anti-climax. It seemed, at first, that even
this, the war that I had been anticipating, yet dreading, all
my life, was not much different from the peace. There
was a dull sense of disbelief but not much more. I don't
know what I expected. Fireworks in the sky? The sweat
and grime of trenches? Hand-to-hand combat? Yes, all of

these. That's not to say I wasn't afraid. Weren't we all? Suddenly items like gas masks, dusty relics of our parents' time, were resurrected, not as triggers for nostalgia but as something real and useful. Although even they seemed antiquated and foolish like treadle sewing-machines or hand-driven mangles.

The bombs dropping here – that made all the difference. I remember the sound of the air-raid sirens in the night, the whistle and thunder of shells and thinking it a bizarre kind of joke. I mean, these things are so familiar now from second-hand, like the conventions of courtship. I, too, had watched war movies. We'd had a few alerts but no one really took them seriously. It couldn't happen, that's what we thought. At least, that's what I thought. It just couldn't happen. It did. That first night 200 died. We've had some skirmishes here in our time – squalid ambushes on the streets, but this was in a different league. I remember walking through the city the morning afterwards. The corpses of missiles like huge, ruined whales. The rubble, smoking still, the naked gable walls left standing, the tangled wreckage of cars – and I loved it. I loved the devastation.

Michael did not feel the same way. A professional soldier, *he* was angry.

'They went for civilian targets,' he said, 'that's against the rules. They're playing dirty . . . '

Even then it was on the tip of my tongue to say to him: 'So are we.'

War gave us an excuse. Be merry, for tomorrow we die. It is tomorrow now and we are alive and well and contributing to the war effort. The War Effort. They have used all the old posters. Lord Kitchener – your country needs you. And that other one about loose talk. The generals are our new nannies. They speak to us in loud declamatory headlines with exclamation marks after them as if by shouting there will be no room for secrets. But every war has its secrets.

The enemy, they tell us, is closer than we think. Any one of us could be the enemy. Hence the admonitions to deceive. Not that we needed much encouragement. There is the confidential telephone into which you can whisper your suspicions. I have often felt tempted to use it. How comforting to speak into the dark about your worst fears, to pass them on to somebody responsible who you know will look after them. Like confession without the judgement. But that's the trouble isn't it? Who knows what you might say in the soothing fog of anonymity with the weighted silence of a trained and avid listener at the other end. No, better to keep one's own counsel.

I have heard them in the dead of night take people off for questioning. A tip-off, they will say, no more. There are muffled conversations on the doorstep, the scrunch of feet on gravel as somebody is led away. The car doors slam, echoing in the empty street. There is the growl of engines and the hiss of tyres and in their wake an eerie, ringing silence. That's all.

I sing to keep my heart up. No, not true, I sing to pay
the rent. *My* contribution to the war effort. We entertain
the troops. We cheer the lads up before we send them off.
Tank them up and get them singing, that's the idea. I'm
a backing-singer with Rennie Fox's All-Star Band. I'm
one of those women in the black dresses who sing 'do-
whap-she-do' in the background. I can do synchronised
movements too. Suddenly, my skills are in demand; the
phone's been hopping. Business was bad before the war.
I was reduced to doing cabaret places – tacky dives where
you double up as a barmaid. Bad news. This is my life
now, I thought, just more of this. And then the war
came. And with it an appetite for romance, at least in
song. They can't get enough of it. Love and surfing –
they're our winners. I shouldn't mock, I suppose. Even
the corniest song has a resonance for somebody, so I just
stand there and mouth my way through them. Don't get
me wrong, I'm glad of the work and I have no ambition
for better. Before the war nobody in the business could
quite believe that I never wanted to be in the spotlight,
out front on stage with the lights pouring down. I have
always been happy in the background; it suits me. But
people suspect you if you're happy with your lot. Or,
at least, they used to. Now there's no time for personal
ambition. We're all involved in bigger work. I, for one,
am relieved. The burden of seeking out a private meaning
for the world was all too much. Now the only meaning
is war.

This woman followed Michael first. It's fair to say she haunted him. I could see it in his face. She made her presence felt in his averted gaze or the way he would pick at the quicks on his fingers. We prided ourselves that there were no secrets between us and at first she – or at least the idea of her – was not a secret. She was there; it's just we never spoke about her. Some day, I would think, some day we'll talk about her, but not just yet. The truth was we felt guilty about our private happiness, not just because of her. We were superstitious too. In the midst of death, *we* were happy.

Of course, I didn't have to face the prospect of sending my man off to war. We are both of us too old. Saved by our age, our job is to keep the home fires burning. Or, in Michael's case, to train the young ones for defeat. How to be a good captive. Survival tactics. The Geneva Convention. Name, rank and serial number. How to withstand torture. Hold out as long as you can, he tells them, that's all that is expected of you.

It was only after a while that I suspected Michael of deliberately harbouring her. He would try to smuggle her into the conversation, just in passing. Her name, alone. Dorothy. I found it a ridiculous name; I laughed at it to myself. It spoke to me of pretension. Dorothy, indeed. I experimented with ludicrous abbreviations. Dots, Dor, Dottie. I don't think he realised in the beginning what a dangerous practice it was to speak of her. The walls have ears. He should have used a code. And there was his position to think about; he could have been accused of consorting with the enemy. The fact of her alone was dangerous. But he was hiding her at home and worse again, had embroiled a civilian – me – in his subterfuge. I wondered where he kept her. In the cellar perhaps, where she would never see the daylight. Or the attic, guarded by a trap door. Or did she live in the body of the house, passed off as some distant relative trapped by the onset of hostilities? A prisoner of war. I didn't ask. I didn't want to know.

I was angry with him. I knew what he wanted. He wanted someone to take her off his hands. The hidden woman. He had not anticipated how difficult it would be to keep her under wraps. It is not even as if she has caused him grief. Even he admits she has behaved impeccably, following all the rules, accepting all the strictures imposed. In as much as she has been able, she has looked after herself. She has asked for little. He readily admits how difficult it has been for her, keeping to the house, being invisible to all intents and purposes. But it seemed after a while, the very goodness of her behaviour was a provocation to him. It made him panicky. Sometimes I thought he might even report her himself. Lift up the phone and make an anonymous call. But no, surely not. He had taken risks for her after all, jeopardised his career, us, to keep her safe. Why would he ruin all that, just to sleep easy in his bed?

I waited for the day when he would ask me to take her on. I would say no, of course. This was his problem, I would reason. He had volunteered for it. The war would not last forever. Sooner or later there would be surrender or defeat. The notion of her winning did not occur to me – then. When he mentioned her I would urge him to talk to her. If she knew how much danger there was in this for him, she would surely not persist. In the last war, people who hid Jews in their houses often only had to express the vaguest unease and they would wake up the following morning to find their basements empty, and the hidden tenants gone. Couldn't the same apply to her, I wondered. But he suspected the worst. He expected a fight. He was right.

It was All Saints Night. A blustery evening. There had been a lull in hostilities leaving the night free for the ghosts of the good to wander free. Michael came from the depot. He left his greatcoat and cap in the hallway as he always did. This was the boundary of our private world. It was one of the things I loved him for, his deference to these unspoken rules. I could say now that I felt her then between us, caught in the tangle of sheets but in fact that isn't true. We were too greedy for happiness to allow that. The only difference that I felt was that when his weight came down on me, it was, for the first time, a dead weight. The weight of two.

She has been with me since. I had imagined that an

interloper would have made her presence felt directly. Moved things about, or that I would have been troubled by voices. But she doesn't speak. She is as silent as the grave. And yet, I know that she is here. Not constantly, mind you. Like Michael she is deferential; she does not impose. For hours at a time she makes herself scarce, the perfect house guest. She's not a prisoner in my home, after all.

I only know she's around because I feel her eyes on everything. She has turned my house into a series of traps. Nothing within these walls is innocent anymore. The table where we've eaten, the debris of our meals – these are charged with meaning. An empty wine bottle is a weapon. His gifts, small things like the travelling-clock or the leather bookmark, leap out at me on mantelpiece and sideboard, slyly detaching themselves from the general flotsam and jetsam of the household. And his belongings, what few he leaves behind him through absent-mindedness – a cigarette lighter, a single glove – these are like sharp recriminations. I feel *her* pangs when I see them.

The bedroom reeks of her. I know that when I'm out she wanders in there and touches things – idly. She is a prowler, not a thief. She has fingered the stuff of my dresses and has tried on my hats (I have a weakness for hats). She has stood in front of *my* mirror tilting the brims this way and that until they sit just right on her. She has dabbled in my perfume. She doesn't wear it; she merely opens the caps and lets the scent escape into the air.

The bed, where doubtless she has lain, looks wanton now, the pillows flung about, the coverlet thrown carelessly back, the sheets a geography of crushed tributaries. Even when I sleep in it alone it looks this way because *her* gaze has made it so.

Michael believes there's an end in sight. He's cheery and optimistic these days. The generals have finally seen sense, he says, and are doing what he privately advocated all along. Hold back on the attack, lay siege and wait for the enemy to make the first move. Driven into a corner they may turn on one another, wild-eyed with hunger and desperate for escape and claw each other's eyes out. Even now supplies are running short. Within the walled city, skeletons wander. Soon, Michael says, they will be begging for mercy.

I am growing thin, a wraith, Michael says. He blames the rationing; they've introduced food coupons. We haven't had red meat for months and fruit is but a memory. Dorothy is more robust, he says, more flesh to lose. He speaks quite freely of her now that he is free of her. He pokes fun at her.

'I hear Dodo's on the prowl,' he says. He calls her Dodo. A pet name. 'Looking for a conquest.'

He can afford to joke about her. She is no threat to him.

But here, the war continues.

MOMENT OF
DOWNFALL

I WAS CAUGHT OFF-GUARD by the invitation to the class reunion. Fifteen years on. That was the first shock. I had swiftly torn up the invites to the fifth and tenth anniversaries without a second thought, so why was this one different? Well, I'm getting older, that's part of it. I've noticed lately how charmed I am to discover that I have known what is obsolete. You know the sort of thing – the brand names of sweets long since cleared off the shelves, forgotten street games, the characters in teenage comics. It's like coming into an unexpected inheritance. But it wasn't nostalgia that made me pause before destroying this little missive from the past. It was the name at the bottom. It was signed Elizabeth Norton (Page). The double surname threw me at first. Like a disguise, it sat there taunting me. Guess who this is, it seemed to say. A roll of drums. Yes folks, the person you've been waiting for, Li-iz . . . Page!

Funny, isn't it, the power of names. They lodge with you long after their owners have disappeared. I can still remember the roll call from High Babies – see how that dates me – the list of girls who sang seconds in the school choir, the rota of supervisors at my first job. Just recently I came across a piece of paper

97

among my things with the names of seventy people on
it. I wondered for a moment why they were all gathered
together like this (had I been making an inventory of
my friends?) until I realised that this was the guest
list for my wedding, the one that didn't happen. I
chickened out at the last minute. But that's another
story. Seeing our names there, Tony's and mine – this
must have been when I was trying to sort out numbers
for the hotel – comforted me, strangely. They spoke of
a full life with a well-defined place for me at the centre
of it. I read through the list aloud; it was like repeating
a mantra, the low hum of the once familiar. It reminded
me of Mrs Bergin's kindergarten. A basement room with
small-paned windows and pocked wooden floorboards,
small feet drumming on the planks and the glorious
discord of tables sung out by forty four-year-olds. We
seemed to have learned everything by chanting. Dick can
run, Mary can run, Spot can run. All eyes on the board,
all together now.

Of course, I know that part of my preoccupation with
other people's names is the anticipation of my own being
celebrated. I imagine, sometimes, that I am famous and
a TV documentary team is going through memorabilia
seeking *my* name out from the crowd, the camera scrolling
down through lists of unknowns or panning out across a
group photograph before settling finally on me. There I
am, in grainy close-up, smiling hopefully, giving no clue
to the germ of greatness within. The fantasy only goes

this far, sadly. I have yet to decide how to make a name for myself.

There was a time when my name had a magical power. When I was a child I used it to hypnotise myself. I would sit in front of the mirror in my room and call my name aloud several times, rocking back and forth until I was no longer inside myself but floating in some high corner of the room, watching myself far below. It was a solitary pleasure, I must admit. I was always afraid that I would crash down before I could smuggle myself back inside again or that my mother or someone else would come in, interrupting the process and leaving me dangling forever in mid-air. It was always a relief to be safely snug within again, but the knowledge that I had the password with which I could spirit myself away at any time was both fearful and exciting.

But where were we? Liz Page. Liz Page was a rangy, attractive girl with the sort of looks which even then – we're talking thirteen here – would bloom spectacularly but would age badly. Oh, the dark eyes would survive, but wouldn't her straight nose sharpen too much when she was older and her thin face become horsey-looking? That was what my mother would say. She meant well, of course or rather, she meant well for me. She recognised the curious mixture of envy and disdain I felt for Liz Page, realising I am sure, my secret and shameful craving to be liked by a girl I did not care for, and for whom my mother did not care out of loyalty to me.

Why was Liz Page so popular? (I feel I have to use
both her names; they sit together as a unit. Liz, alone,
would seem bereft, powerless.) Well, I suppose, she was
good-looking, she was thin, she had a place on the hock-
ey team – these things were important then. She had the
knack of always being the centre of attention. The others
seemed to gravitate towards her. I never saw her walking
on the corridor alone; she was always with a gang that
strode along four abreast forcing girls like me to hug
the wall. On the tennis courts or in the classroom if
there was a huddle of girls together, it was always
around Liz Page. She was tall for her age. She had
the coveted job of opening the sash windows and in
school photographs she was always in the dead centre of
the back row, the anchor around which the tableau was
built. She misbehaved, but in a sly way – lots of face-
pulling and note passing – and she rarely got caught. In
this way she neatly saved herself from being considered a
goody-goody, not only by us, but by teachers too. They
distrusted consistent good behaviour as much as we did.
They liked girls with spirit, they said, and Liz Page's
capacity to bluff her way through questions (she skimped
on homework) never failed to disarm them. She had, my
mother asserted in her defence, a good manner. That was
because she always had a bright hello for my mother on
the street while I shuffled past *her* mother, resentful and
defiantly shy.

Perhaps I was the enemy for Liz Page in the same way as

she was for me. She must have distrusted my fat glumness and sensed the secret spite in my heart. My dogged brand of bookishness might well have daunted her but it seemed to me then – and still does now – a poor substitute for her coltish grace, her long-limbed ease, her shallow but endearing charm. The truth is there have always been Liz Pages for me. They follow me, surround me. I look for them. Whereas she has doubtless shrugged me off; she would probably have to be prompted to remember my name.

I was curious, of course, about the reunion I wouldn't go to. I wondered what they would look like. All I could imagine were their little girl faces superimposed on women's bodies. They would get dressed up (their sense of competition would not have deserted them) but they wouldn't overdo it. The rules of teenage mating would still apply. You *never* wore your best. And now, as then, those who came too hopefully in clothes that advertised their newness would be silently despised. The evening's events would go something like this. Firstly, there would be Mass in the oratory, then tea and sandwiches in the convent, where we would be expected to mingle with the few aged nuns who still remain and still remember us. There would be some polite oohing and aahing as we rediscovered one another. The sense of occasion would not allow us to descend into girlish shrieking (that would come later). Then Sister Xavier, still living, I believe, would clap her hands peremptorily and call for a short silence for those who could not be with us – surely death has claimed its youthful percentage? I toyed with the notion that my absence might be counted as a death of sorts. I imagined what they might say. Poor Della, that's what they would say, which is probably what they'd say about me anyway, dead or alive. Then we would be led through The Nuns' Corridor (the geography of the place, its names, they haunt me too) to the assembly hall. Liz Page would deliver a suitably chummy speech with just the right amount of sentiment so that we could stand surrounded by the props of our youth – the creaky stage, the battered piano, the vaulting horse – and sink into a brief, dreamy, manufactured sadness. And later, of course, there would be drinks in a pub, a meal, and the girls would let their hair down. At some stage in the night, late, probably just before she was about to leave, Liz Page would turn to me and with a jubilant insincerity would enquire: Well, Della, how's life been treating you?

That would be my moment, wouldn't it? Where would I start? The moment of downfall is always good. The year is 1970. We are in our first year of secondary school. It is early summer. High blue skies and drowsy afternoons, a time when the world seems to offer the gift of endless days. There is an air of levity about – these days have forgotten the gravity of winter and the solemn start to the school year. The nuns, overheated in their dark habits, are red-faced and slightly comical. The lay teachers – Mr

Crawford for Latin, Miss Busby for French – resort to jokiness or snap their books shut with ten minutes to go and send us home early. In case she doesn't remember, I will remind Liz Page that this was the year Sister Baptist was sent to the missions and Mr Crawford taught her to drive on the playground. He had a low-powered motorbike which he used to ply his trade between us and the boys' college three miles away. He travelled, goggled and helmeted and swaddled in waterproofs. A nervous Sister Baptist sat astride the machine – we thought she might ride side-saddle – and chugged her way across the forecourt of the school with Mr Crawford taking up the rear on foot. We could hear the drone of the engine from our classroom and during break-time we would watch the lessons mirthfully from the upper windows. Sister Baptist, her veil fluttering under a red globe and wearing Mr Crawford's outsized anorak, manfully revved at the controls and struck down on the kick pedal with a polite foot. The machine would suddenly judder into life, shooting forward like a sprinter from the blocks only to stall moments later and come to a grinding standstill. Mr Crawford, a big-boned, solid man, would mime the actions for her repeatedly, crouched ape-like, legs apart and knees bent, one foot pawing the air, his thick fingers clenching and opening in demonstration. There was much mounting and dismounting, which we found hilarious, and once or twice she rode pillion, her hands lightly clasping his burly waist as he did nifty figures-of-eight across the tar. Liz Page will certainly remember this. She was the one who led the raucous band of spectators.

The round of petty thieving started around that time. They were trinkety things at first – hair slides, combs, a bracelet. Then Esther Bailey's watch was taken during gym, followed quickly by Denise Harding's fountain pen; within a week, Sheila Downey's purse, Babs Riordan's hockey-stick and Mary Ferry's ballet shoes had all disappeared. The final straw was when someone – 'someone' was a character that would, in time, gain resonance for all of us – someone stole Cathy Butler's locket from her shoe cage. She had buried it in one of her runners during play rehearsal and when she came back it was gone. The locket belonged to Cathy's mother who had died when she was a baby and this was her only memento. How melodramatic it all sounds but true, nevertheless. A tear-streaked Cathy and the ghost of her long-dead mother (the story was she died having Cathy) hovered magnificently in our midst. Something, Sister Xavier declared, would have to be done. We were, she went on, in the presence of a cruel and heartless thief.

I remember how excited this made me feel, as if we were on the verge of a great adult discovery.

'Until the thief (enunciated with glamorous emphasis) owns up, all of you are under suspicion.'

Lessons were suspended. We were all to be punished, we were told, until the guilty one confessed. At first it did not seem like punishment. In fact, we couldn't believe our luck. For once it was perfectly acceptable to stare off into the blue mid-distance, or lapse into a lazy reverie unchecked. But, after a few hours, the enforced idleness made us twitchy. We sat in the classroom while Sister Xavier paced up and down between the rows, her large, age-spotted hands toying with the hems of her capacious sleeves. Sun streamed through the windows; from below we could hear the lazy pock of tennis balls and the desultory cries of 'love', 'love 15'. This, particularly, reinforced our sense of being stranded in the middle of our own drama; as in the midst of grief, life around us continued on as normal. The bell rang out to mark the change of classes, followed by the clattery hubbub of droves of girls in transit on the echoing corridors. For five minutes we relished the institutional clamour outside our door, then the bell would go again, doors would slam, and an eerie silence would descend.

I have to admit that there were parts of it I enjoyed. Our crime – at that stage it belonged to all of us – made us gleam with danger. 'Are you in 1A?' girls would ask, rushing up, girls who would normally have ignored me. Or they would camp outside our door ready to pounce on any fresh news. Even Sarah Kinnell, a fifth-year who was tipped to be the next head girl, (alas, she never made it; she got pregnant that summer) took me aside on the corridor and whispered: 'Is it true that Laura Daly did it?' So this, I thought, is what it's like to be popular, to be in demand. It was like walking among magnets; I had to *do* nothing.

I knew, of course, that like me, it was the notoriety attached to the thieving that mesmerised them and made them envious, and that once the thief confessed she would replace me in the hypnotic glare of their attention. But while it lasted I savoured it.

Liz Page thought the whole thing was a hoot. That was one of her expressions. She didn't take it seriously, or at least, not in the way I did.

'You'd want to be nuts to steal things from around here. Shops would be much better,' she said as we filed out of class after our second day of confinement. 'Anyway, who on earth would want Mary Ferry's stinky ballet shoes?'

She hadn't been listening to a word Sister Xavier had said, I thought crossly. It wasn't the things themselves the thief was after. What kleptomaniacs crave is attention; they desperately want to be noticed.

On the third day I tried to get out of it. I told my mother I had a headache, which was true, but it was only the same thudding dread that accompanied most of my mornings before school.

'What's this in aid of?' she asked suspiciously as she pinned up her hair. I'd left it too late; she was ready to go to work. She used to dress on the run. I'd often seen her in her stockinged feet in front of the mirror in the kitchen wriggling into a skirt or pulling a sweater on while I had my breakfast. Similarly when she came in from work she would tear off her tights as if she were being let out of harness, or extricate her bra down the sleeves of her dress muttering 'God, this thing is killing me!' My mother had very few private moments.

'Well?' she asked.

I was already ashamed of this feeble attempt. My mother demanded physical evidence – a roaring temperature or a raw throat – before she'd keep me out of school. Any sickness threatened to topple the fragile routine of the household.

She packed me off with two aspirins (in case it got worse later on) knowing that I wouldn't take them. I had difficulty swallowing tablets; they always ended up as gritty meal in my mouth. And I wouldn't admit at school that I needed a spoonful of jam to help the medicine go down.

'Wait till you grow up,' she said, 'then you'll know what headaches are.'

It was a scorching day. The room smelt of fresh sweat and stale fear. We had the jaded air of refugees or survivors of a shipwreck, nerves jangling but dull-eyed from the tedium of the flat, open sea. We had long since given up hope of catching sight of land. It was as if this was what our life had always been. The school sports were on that day. From the playing-fields we could hear the rowdy baying of those let loose. Their freedom taunted us, cooped up in our classroom. The school was deserted, the corridors tinged with the melancholy ache of an unpeopled public place. When we were let out to go to the toilet – always in twos – the emptiness forced us to whisper as if we were somewhere sacred and forbidden.

At noon Sister Xavier ordered Liz Page to open the windows as far as they would go – Susan Gilbert had fallen asleep at her desk and Frances Cahill was feeling faint and had to sit with her head between her knees. The waft of a breeze, the buzzing of summer, the distant roar of the crowd infused us with a new alertness.

Sister Xavier, who had been sitting on the podium reading her office, her lips moving silently in prayer, rose and went to the open windows.

'There is,' she said finally, addressing the cloudless sky as if she were talking to God out there, 'someone among us who desperately needs help.' She paused, then turned around scanning our faces, until her gaze fell on me.

'Someone who does not feel loved.'

The word sent a titter of embarrassed glee through the room. I felt my cheeks colour. Yes, I thought fiercely, there is.

'Someone whom we overlook, perhaps, someone whom we do not notice,' she crooned softly. I remember when my mother used to talk to me like this.

'Someone who isn't top of the class or captain of the team, whose gifts and talents we have failed to recognise . . . '

Yes, I thought, she knows, she understands.

'Someone who is calling out . . . '

I could feel my lip quiver and incriminating tears well in my eyes. If I didn't get out soon I would end up crying – in front of the whole class. I couldn't bear it; I had to stop her before it was too late. I rose to my feet.

'Yes, Della?'

I looked around me. For one intoxicating moment I felt the rapt stillness of their full attention. I saw in their faces, shock, awe, a grudging respect. I was going to save them all, and one in particular. I could feel them willing me to speak. Go on, they urged silently, go on, do it.

'Sister, I . . .' I faltered even then. 'I have something to confess.'

I have long ago worked out that it must have been Liz Page. I mean, it's obvious, isn't it? Who among us sought out attention more than she, always in a crowd, the teachers' pet, the classroom hero. She was bound to get drunk on all that popularity and it must have made her greedy for more. Think how it would have ruined her if she had been unmasked as a thief; some of her friends would never have got over it. Her mother would have been devastated. My mother used to say darkly that all was not well in the Page household. Liz, she would say, Liz has her problems too. How right she was.

'You, of all people, Della,' Sister Xavier said after she had dismissed the class. 'And your poor mother, it'll break her heart. First your father, and now this . . . '

My father had died the summer before. A drowning accident. A rip tide. My mother and I watched from the beach as he went down. We heard him call out but there was nothing we could do. He had ignored the red flag. It took them days to find the body. It had been swept out to sea. My mother and I went to the beach every day. She would scan the horizon as if somehow he might still be out there waving to us. She wouldn't let them remove his heap of clothing from the shoreline. As long as they were there, she felt he might come back for them. Anyway, she said to me, that's all we have of him now . . .

'And what did you do with Cathy Butler's locket?' Sister Xavier asked.

'I threw it away.'

That was when I had to start lying.

'But why, Della, why?'

I shrugged. What could I say?

She looked at me sorrowfully and shook her head. 'Poor Della,' she said. 'Poor Della.'

It was the making of me, really, you could say. The reputation of petty thievery dogged me long after the brief glory of confessing had faded away. And long-term notoriety, I found, was less spectacular. The others were wary of me; they shied away from talking to me. Nothing new in that except that it was accompanied by a new watchfulness. They circled around me although it was they who were afraid that I might swoop, not the other way round. And *that* had its own power. Not unlike being able to hypnotise myself, a knack I subsequently lost. (I found my name could no longer render me light and invisible; it had become a heavy, grounded thing.) The only other difference was that they hid things from me, their bright glittery things that is, as if I were a magpie unable to resist the dazzle.

I have Sharon to blame for the marriage that didn't happen. Sharon at the hairdressers. I never knew her surname. They don't tell you the stylists' second names; that way it seems like they're friends of yours. Chatty Sharon cut my hair on the morning of the wedding.

'This lady's getting married today,' she announced to the salon, beaming.

Several red-faced women trapped under the driers nodded stiffly and smiled.

'A white wedding,' she said, 'isn't that lovely!'

I sat in front of the mirror, dripping. I always feel at my plainest at this point. Slicked down hair and a splotchy face from the wash, or is it the lights in these places?

'I think it's wonderful,' Sharon confided, 'that people get married, I mean. Biggest day of your life, my mother says, a girl never forgets her wedding-day. It's her day, really, isn't it, the bride's . . . ?'

She started to snip at the tails round my ears.

'I don't believe people should live together before-hand. I'm not a prude, mind you, but it's so much more romantic, I think, making your vows at the altar.'

I tried to tune out of the chatter. I wondered if it would be very rude to ask for a magazine.

'It makes it more real, doesn't it, going public like that. Standing up in front of all those people and saying "I do".'

I felt a sudden shiver.

'I mean to say it's easy to live in sin because nothing is expected of you. Nobody's to know what you've prom-ised. But if you get married, now that's different.'

She was on my fringe. I could feel the jaws of the scissors near my temple though I had my eyes firmly shut.

'Then you're telling the world, aren't you?'

She tilted my head to the left. It made me look quizzical.

'You've said you'll love, honour and obey in front of everybody . . . '

She was working somewhere near the nape of my neck now. I always think of that part of me as being the most secret, so defenceless and untouched. I could feel the cold metallic click of Sharon's scissors. She was concentrating, I could tell. Just as well, one slip and I could have been ruined.

'Now, my fella, Eddie, he just won't have it. Won't commit himself, know what I mean? You'd think I was asking him to admit to a crime the way he goes on.'

She sighed heavily, as she fluffed up the top of my hair with a bunched fist.

'Afraid of getting caught, that's him.'

She looked at me sourly in the mirror for a moment, then remembered herself.

'Now,' she said brightly, 'let's get you under the lights!'

As for Liz Page, she has thrived by all accounts. Not that I follow her career or anything but I hear about her on the grapevine. I know she worked for a bit in the bank and then she got married. I know they have three children, two sons and a daughter. A nice size for a family. That's what we would have had, Tony and I. First there would be Anthony (called after his father), then Colin, and Rachel for the girl. I've always liked that name, Rachel . . . it has a ring to it. I see a fair, willowy girl, full of grace and humour, a much-loved last child. In my dream I am standing in an airy house waiting for the sound of her step in the hallway brimming with that secretive mother-love that displaces all others. I expect her home at any minute. I am filled with the promise of her arrival. How different things would have been if I'd been a Rachel . . .

INVISIBLE
MENDING

A cell, two chairs, a table. The suspect (female) and the interrogator (male).

Buddy strikes the table with his fist. His armpits are wet. Old sweat stains are clearly visible on his shirt like the froth-edged hems of jellyfish. He paces up and down, hands resting on his paunch, strands of hair slicked down on his glistening pate.

'Be reasonable, my sweet.'

He indulges himself with endearments as if gorging on rich chocolate. He draws his chair back scraping it along the floor, sits down and clasping his small hands together, gazes at the suspect. His expression is one of reproachful candour.

'Look, love,' – he positively paws the word – 'we're not going to hurt you. I have a daughter your age, for God's sake.'

Pardner tries to imagine a daughter of Buddy's and fails.

'I wouldn't like to see her in a mess like this.'

Buddy shakes his head mournfully; he is convincing, he always turns in a good performance. Women fall for it – on the job, anyway. Outside? Who knows? Prefers boys, Pardner suspects.

'All we need's your signature.'

Buddy wheedles beautifully. He makes them feel guilty, as if they had wounded him personally.

'Why don't you confess – we know all about it. We have it all written down . . . you must be tired.' He adds this with an admirably plausible kindness. 'It's been days now. Think of a nice warm bed, clean sheets . . . sleep!'

Buddy's performance pivots on certain words. He rises, does one quick turn of the cell and then he's back leaning across the table, crushing her face in his fist.

'OK, my lovely, if that's the way you want it.'

He opens his belt and slowly draws it out of the loops around his waist.

'It's very sharp,' he says pointing to the buckle with a viper's smile. The suspect (Pardner never knows their names; it's a policy of his) is already softening. He can tell from the defeated hunch of her shoulders and the way she runs her hands distractedly through her hair. She straightens as Buddy approaches, her fists clenched against her temples to shut out the drumming sound of her own fear. Buddy stands, the leather lolling in his hand. He sighs the sigh of a reluctant tyrant, the man victimised by duty. She is on the brink of surrender. She is about to turn her life over to Pardner. Only he can save her now.

One green canvas bag containing the following. One jar of lip salve; two Biros – one black, one blue. The blue one has leaked. See, Pardner points out, see how all the ink has clogged up at the far end and has seeped out into a corner of the bag leaving a stain shaped like a . . . but, he shrugs, this is irrelevant. One travel pass; one address book, one packet of cigarettes; one hairbrush; one map of the city; one flyer for 'Save the Seals'; three small coins – foreign; one brown plastic wallet containing £2.39 in cash and three postage stamps; one box of matches from The Horse and Tram, a public house; one chipped button. From a summer dress, Pardner guesses. It is small and shell-like. He sees the dress it came from. Navy blue with puff sleeves and smocking at the breast. The button pops one day in the garden when she stretches to unpeg washing from the line. He imagines the dry crush of sheets against her cheek as she stoops, with a basket of sun-dried laundry in her arms, to rescue it from the uncut grass. She puts the button in her pocket and then transfers it to her bag so that she won't lose it. But seasons pass, one and then another. She begins to wonder if she ever really liked that dress – the waist was never right and the shoulders didn't sit well. She keeps the button though; it nestles in a seam of the bag like a fossil; it's a kind of good luck charm, a

hansel for the bag. In time it becomes more precious than
the dress . . . but, says Pardner, I digress.

These are Pardner's raw materials. He spills them on to
the table and spreads them out so nothing is obscured
from view. He picks each item up and turns it over in
his hand to get a feel for its owner. Our things, he says,
our personal effects tell tales on us. When we're around
they sit there playing dead, but once we turn our backs
they come alive. Remember, he says, the story about the
magic toyshop where the toys came alive when the lights
went out. (Pardner liked this story as a child. He liked
to think his toys indulged in play while he was sleeping.
They had such little fun with him. He bullied them and
tore their eyes out.) Adult possessions, he will tell you,
are just the same; they have a secret life which bristles
with incrimination.

He used to watch his mother go through pockets.
Wash-day Mondays in the steaming kitchen. She was
proud of that machine, the first one on the street, a
pea-green, tub-like contraption with a wringer on the
top – two leering black rollers set in a pair of iron jaws
through which their clothes were fed as if to a greedy
god. She sorted the laundry out in variegated piles on the
floor. Whites, heavy soils, coloureds. She would fish his
father's shirts out of the plastic linen basket, their palsied
arms hanging over the rim like ravaged corpses, feeling
in them for loose change – coins fouled up the machine's

works – or hunted through his pants pockets not just for money but for any general salvage. Washers, keys, tickets, receipts – she sifted through these and speculated on them. Why did Tom have a penknife in the back pocket of his shorts? What was a note from Irene Waters doing in Dominic's overalls? She read letters shamelessly. Smells and stains, too, she deciphered.

'He's been to the pub,' she would cry with bitter triumph, sniffing at one of her son's sweaters. 'This reeks of cigarette smoke.'

'What's this?' she would ask, eyes narrowing, her face crushed into his father's shirt before tossing it in Pardner's direction for a second opinion. 'Engine oil, I'd swear. Doing nixers on the sly.'

The half-glimpsed thing, the implication, the shadow of a doubt – on these she thrived. She needed not to know but to suspect. Or so Pardner thought.

The kitchen was her domain. It is there Pardner remembers her, scooping flour from a white enamel bin or rolling pastry out on the red formica table with its stork-like tubular legs, marking out perfect circles in the dough with a floury glass. Or reaching up to the impossibly high presses with vents in their doors like coats-of-arms. They snapped shut with an angry click at the slightest provocation – often no more than a tap from an overextended Mrs Pardner showing bare leg at the top of her stockings. Almost everything she did smacked of punishment. She marched into rooms grim-faced with work and bullied them. She would scowl at books on the floor or round on a stray sock as if it might bite her. An open drawer would be thwacked shut, the curtains yanked across as if they should know their place and hadn't she warned them? At night she used to wash her hair in the kitchen sink, turning in the collar of her dress and baring her neck like a victim for the guillotine, before plunging her head into the basin. She rubbed and scrubbed and scratched like one possessed while gobbets of froth quivered on her shoulders or slithered off her shoes. To see her bent double at the sink, her arm wildly grasping for the towel was like witnessing the panicked moments before a drowning. But she always re-emerged, sleek and black as an otter, wrapping the towel into a turban around her dripping head, a penitent rising from the river.

Pardner is standing in the corridor outside the detention room watching through the pane of glass set high in the door. These are the slowed-up moments before damage is done. The suspect is sobbing. Buddy towers over her, silent and menacing. The air ticks with fear, the world steeped in the bleached clarity of dawn. Pardner remembers how it was – the debris of a room where a drunken man has supped, the wordless woman desperate to appease. The fire has died to a few glowing embers, the room is turning cold. His father sinking into a jittery sleep; his mother waiting for his breathing to steady. She rises gingerly from the chair, leaning on the table with her fists. His father shudders suddenly and opens a bleary eye.

'And where do you think you're going?'

He lumbers to his feet and catches her by the wrist. She is always surprised by his sudden shows of deftness.

'Hah! Going to run off, were we?'

In the next room, the boy that was Pardner wakes to a familiar sense of foreboding. He has learned to read the silences. He climbs out of bed and creeps to the door. It is always left ajar – he is afraid of the dark still – and his mother leaves the light on in the kitchen. At night he can hear her at her chores. It comforts him to go to sleep to the clatter of delft or the hiss of the iron, as if the household were a boiler that his mother labours to keep stoked. Through the slit in the door he sees the ruined kitchen, his father's raised fist, his mother's hand shielding her eyes. He rushes out into the light.

'Stop!' he commands. His father, alarmed by the intrusion, lets his hand drop lumpenly to his side. His mother, backing off, looks ashamed. No one knows what to do next. But the small boy in the rumpled pyjamas has discovered the power of having averted something large and dangerous with just a word . . .

'Ah, Pardner,' Buddy says looking up, 'the very man!'

The suspect was picked up at the Hotel Slovak, an immigrant dump on the southern line. Pardner stayed in one himself when he first came – sagging beds, smell of socks, snoring through the night. Aliens Section raids these places from time to time. They always pick up a few strays, illegals, petty thieves, dope smokers. This one, though, was clean as a whistle. Passport in order, even a work permit. Nothing in her room to speak of – a holdall, a couple of spy novels (Pardner notes this wryly), a pocket radio, a can of air freshener wedged under the sash window to keep it open. A few snapshots. Blurred, off-centre pictures of couples with their arms thrown around each other, beer cans raised to the camera and the same cramped bedroom in the background. A dole card on the bedside locker. Fellow on the desk said she kept herself to herself; tabloid shorthand for a killer.

This is how Pardner imagines her last day of freedom. She rises late, maybe noon. She spends less money that way and it's easier to keep warm in bed. It is November. Mornings are blue-cold and smoggy. Wearing a towelling-robe gone bald at the arse, she ducks down the corridor to the bathroom. She washes her hair. The water is lukewarm. The towel she uses is thin and undersized. As she dresses she listens to the tinny radio, mouthing the words of pop songs. She pulls on a pair of jeans and an overlarge pullover. She is careless about her appearance like someone distracted by bereavement or haunted by an impossible love. She gropes blindly under the bed for shoes. She has only two pairs. Yesterday her boots got soaked in a downpour and are packed with newspaper, a home remedy, echo of a former life. So she has to wear her sandals, a plastic pair which look odd with her thick socks. But the day is dry and she hasn't far to go. Before she leaves she shakes the can of air freshener and sprays the room. There is a smell in it she cannot shift, a mixture of damp and cat piss, though she can't trace the source of either. Little wonder, Pardner thinks, *this* is the smell of poverty. She steps out on to the street and immediately rummages in her bag for her map. It is a reflex action, a kind of armour. The map is well-thumbed, dirty along the folds. Certain train stations are circled on it. In the first few weeks she found the trains impossible. She regularly wound up going in the wrong direction or missing connections. She walks down the high street. Smells of cooking drift in the air. The shops have awnings, their goods in serried rows on crates on the pavement. Foreigners, Pardner notes, like to live like this, huddled and crowded, one step from the street. As she descends into the station a pale young man in a raincoat thrusts a leaflet into her hand. She pushes it unread into her bag. She takes the northbound from Platform 2. She watches people as she travels. Indeed, she has a tendency to stare. She has yet to acquire the commuter's glazed eye. She still expects to see somebody she knows although since she arrived in the city she has never once seen a familiar face. She alights three stops later and makes her way to The Horse and Tram. It is a dim, drear place. The carpet bristles underfoot from years of dried-in spillages. The pop-eyed game machines chime like overused doorbells. She meets a man there, a boyfriend, maybe. He wears a duffel-coat and rolls his own cigarettes. They don't talk much. There is a gloomy solidarity about their companionship as if a shared ordeal were all they had in common. A brush with death, perhaps.

Pardner nearly died when he was nineteen, of a burst appendix. He remembers it as if it had happened to someone else. Well, he was someone else then, a bony, freckled youth with a wiry but unhealthy strength. It was like an attack, perpetrated by an unseen assailant from behind. And when he swung around to retaliate, there was a blinding light in his eyes as if he were about to be interrogated. But no, the time for questions was past; his enemy had turned to torture. There was a flaming pain in his belly as if something were being torn from him. No, no that was later, on the table. First a stretcher ride; an unbroken horse. A blue and wailing journey through the night . . .

It was a useless thing that nearly killed him, a wishbone without a function. Draw the short end and you're dead. For days his mother kept vigil, sitting with him in the white room of death while he drowsed between bouts of alert pain. Her watchfulness disturbed him. It reminded him of another convalescence, a childhood accident. Pardner, lying on two chairs pushed together in front of the fire, nursing a bandaged hand while his mother darned, one hand splayed beneath the woollen wound, the other whipping the air impatiently, threading a fretwork across gaping elbows. Invisible mending. Nobody, Pardner laments, does that anymore.

After the operation he stopped going to the cinema. He was no longer able to suspend his disbelief. He found he could only see what was going on behind the scenes. A pair of lovers on a rumpled bed, kissing hungrily, the music soaring and all Pardner could see was that the wall behind the bed was a cardboard screen, the bedroom a cordoned-off piece of studio, and that just out of sight was the surgical sprawl of camera equipment, a maze of flex and wire, a crew in baseball caps chewing gum and a director with a clipboard shouting 'Cut!' . . .

Watch carefully, Pardner says, this is how it's done. It's not so much a trick as a way of looking. He illustrates. The holding-centre where he works looks out on to one of those sad, neglected city streets that has been overlooked in the grander scheme of things. It is a cobbled street. At one end is a stone railway bridge. A row of sturdy plane trees line the path. Behind them is an open space, the forecourt of a swimming baths, a scarred, red-bricked, municipal establishment. On certain grey days when Pardner takes a break from his work and goes to the window it seems to him that this street belongs somewhere else. Somewhere in Eastern Europe. Warsaw, Budapest, Prague. He doesn't know why. He has never been to any of these places and yet, this fragment of city, this conjunction of stone and leaf and sky makes him believe that he is elsewhere. It doesn't last, of course, this fleeting impression, but it never fails to satisfy. It sends a bleak shiver of excitement through him as if somehow he had cheated on the world as given and glimpsed a second world beneath the surface of the first.

First, he says, we find the suspect; then we choose the crime. Consider me a matchmaker, he says. In this case he has decided that the suspect is a conspirator. Some are lone assassins acting with a heedless kind of daring for which afterwards they are secretly envied. But, he decides, she is not one of those. She has more the mien of a dutiful accomplice, in keeping with her air of cowed obligation. Pardner, in merciful mood, grants her this gift of moral exemption, before he weaves together his conspiracy.

The Hotel Slovak, the perfect cover for a woman on a secret mission. Full of others like herself, losers, nondescripts. That is why she lies in bed till noon, literally under cover, so that afterwards no one will be quite able to place her. Remember, Pardner admonishes, what the desk clerk said. Kept herself to herself. The map is another giveaway. Bombers mark their maps. They ring their targets, identify escape routes. And note, he goes on, how watchfully she travels, waiting for the hand of the law to fall, or checking out the enemy. He leafs through her address book. For new arrivals addresses are a form of currency. Hoarded, traded, bartered. The suspect has very few. She is, in *their* terms, almost destitute. Perhaps, he ventures, she doesn't need to make friends. She is, after all, here to do a job and then to disappear. The man she meets in the pub. Pardner has him checked out. A compatriot, of course. Down on his luck. A graduate working on a building site. No record. Another blameless life. Spends his spare time working for the Animal Redemption League. All things bright and beautiful and all that lark. They write letters, lobby politicians, pleading for the tusks of elephants and the blubber of whales. They picket laboratories protesting against experimentation on rabbits. They favour sit-ins. They like to march and chant, or form human chains. But lately, there have been threats . . . That pocket radio in her room, the perfect size, he notes, for small explosives. Take out the batteries and hey presto! It could nestle unnoticed in the pocket of a fur coat in any large department store. And the air freshener. If this were a bomb factory, Pardner explains, our friend (he has to call her something) would need to get rid of the smell of explosives. Gelignite smells like marzipan. Did you know that, Pardner asks. The Save the Seals leaflet – a foolish blunder, carrying around her own propaganda as if she weren't quite convinced. And then there are her shoes. It is mid-winter yet she is as ill-shod as a Franciscan. Pink plastic. Too pure to wear pig-hide. He hates her kind, soft, ill-formed women who 'care' about dumb animals. Spare us, Pardner says, spare us from inheriting the meek . . .

His father was found lying dead in a puddle on the

street, some of it of his own making, on a dank November night, leaves in his mouth, a great white expanse of
belly showing where his shirt buttons had given way. His
mother waited all night for him to come home. Pardner
found her in the morning, sitting hunched and shivering
at the kitchen-table still keeping an ear out for his key in
the door and his crashing about in the hall. The fire had
gone out and she was stiff with cold and yet she sat,
transfixed by waiting. For the policeman's knock.

She still waits – in a nursing home which Pardner pays
for. She has retreated into silence, wakening only occasion-
ally into querulous complaint or long-lost interrogatives
from conversations years old. She will start suddenly and
fixing him with her glowering gaze she will call out:

'And just *what* is this?' or '*Where* were you?'

She eyes Pardner suspiciously as if he might suddenly
turn on her. As she did once on him.

EXHIBIT C:

A Monday morning. Pardner came home early from
school, picking his way across the sud-streaked yard and
under the sad, dripping lines of washing. Later, he knew,
his mother would walk among the flapping sheets, the
frantic shirts, trying to catch them between her fingers to
see if they were dry, and, Pardner felt, envying them for
their gift of tethered flight. He slipped into the house by
the back door. She did not hear him over the din of the

machine. She was standing by the tub, her apron pocket bulging with clothes pegs. By her side, the laundry basket spilled out its unwashed offal. Pardner's dressing-gown was crumpled under her arm and in her hand she held his pocket diary. (He was foolish enough then to keep written records.) Pardner's schoolboy code of honour contained just two mortal sins – one was murder, the other was reading someone else's diary. He watched, sickened, as she turned the pages over. He was her favourite, the baby of the family, and all those years as her accomplice had made him think that he was, somehow, exempt from her sly scrutiny.

Sensing someone in the room she looked up with a mild sense of surprise.

'If you leave it lying around what do you expect?' She shrugged and stretched out a hand to halt the machine.

The silence thrummed with Pardner's shame and anger.

'You, you . . . you' he stammered jabbing a finger at her.

Her face darkened.

'Don't you point your finger at me, young man!' She said this in her normal cross mother's voice and then, suddenly, she was screaming at him, 'Don't you dare!' and lunging across the machine she grabbed at him. The wringer's jaws were open. She caught his hand and shoved his finger in-between the rollers, snapping the jaws shut and pressing the button to its highest throttle. There was a sickening crunch of flesh and bone . . .

he woke up minus the first two joints of his index finger.

After a few days he was sent home. The doctors were amazed he healed so quickly. Almost mended, they said. Almost. His mother ordered a taxi to bring him from the hospital, an uncharacteristic extravagance. It was a large, black, high-bellied car. They sat in the roomy back, acres of leather between them, and his mother slid across the glass pane that separated them from the driver. He thought this was a signal. Now, she would admit to him what she had done. Instead she clutched her handbag to her breast and said: 'You can never be too careful. Some of these drivers are bogus, you know.'

His father, carrying in his belongings when they arrived at the house grumbled about the cost of the cab.

'You'd have the lad come home on the bus, I suppose,' she said laying her hand on Pardner's shoulder. 'Don't you understand, he's a sick boy.'

He could not credit her silence. Soon, soon, he would think, soon she will speak. There were days in the darkened kitchen, his mother moving among the landscape of laundry, the machine trembling behind her when he was convinced she would confess. To him, to him alone, that was all he wanted. A word to him alone. But the moments of imminent disclosure seemed always to pass like stormclouds overhead, or they were shattered by his father bellowing from another room or a neighbour calling at the door. And in time he had to struggle to remember that he owned another version of the story, particularly when she repeated hers so often.

'The little fool,' she would say, recounting what had now become a family anecdote. 'Put his hand in the machine when my back was turned. Wanted to see how the thing worked, if you don't mind!'

It became a party piece.

Do you remember the day Lennie put his finger in the wringer – a merry peal of laughter here – and then, of all things, turned the damn thing on. Yes, Pardner nods, yes, I remember . . .

'Okay, Buddy, that's enough.'

Buddy drops the belt noisily on the table. The suspect, wet-cheeked, looks up at Pardner gratefully. He puts a consoling hand on her shoulder.

'I think we're ready now, we're ready to sign, aren't we?'

She nods dumbly at him.

'It's all there, ready and waiting . . . '

He places the confession reverently in front of her – it is a precious thing – and uncapping his fountain-pen hands it to her. She sniffles noisily, rubbing her nose with a grimy hand. He looks down at his own severed finger. Every so often it still troubles him – the pain of a phantom limb.

The suspect (our friend, Pardner insists) thumbs through the pages of the confession.

'But, but . . . ' she objects, 'none of this is true. I never . . . It's all lies.'

'No,' Pardner corrects, 'not lies.'

He is offended. He has spent hours producing this seamless work, weaving a story out of her gaping inconsistent life. Who does the snivelling little bitch think she is? He is saving her, doesn't she realise?

'Buddy!' he commands.

Buddy lifts his hand and smartly clouts her, a swift well-aimed chop under the nose that will not bruise the skin but breaks several blood vessels. A stream spurts from her nostrils. Pardner hands her his handkerchief to staunch the flow. Her pinched, shocked face regards him.

'Must I sign this?' she asks weakly.

Pardner loves this moment just before capitulation. He feels a surge of victory tinged with a compelling kindness.

'Yes,' he says, 'I'm afraid you must.'

She lifts her reluctant hand and signs her name in an untidy schoolgirl scrawl. There is blood on her soiled coat.

'I'm glad,' Pardner says, gathering up his papers, 'I'm glad you saw things my way.'

A MARRIAGE OF CONVENIENCE

JUDITH WROTE HER first postcard from the airport at San Quistador. The arrivals area was like the white tunnel between life and death described by people who have 'clinically' died. She sat in one of the yellow plastic bucket seats, the baggage carousel juddering by like a drugged invalid as she scribbled a wistful note to Malcolm. Like everything else between them it was touched by the long finger of yearning. Her other postcards would be bright and pithy, reading something like this: 'Skies of burning blue. Heat – Turkish. Have been to the markets. Bought a huge leather bag. Dead cheap. Also an exotic plant with tongues of red in its leaves called – would you believe it – Lovers' Revenge!'

It was the ideal form of communication; excitement by implication. She couldn't afford to be that jocose with Malcolm.

'My God,' he had said, 'what are you going *there* for? They're slaughtering one another in the streets.'

It was the sort of testy protest that had become a substitute for other declarations. It was an exaggeration, of course. The war had been over for two years now. The country was crying out for European tourists. All the same, the choice of El Quistador was not entirely coincidental. Her holidays had become for Judith primarily a matter of judicious risk. The merest tang of danger was enough.

At last her upended suitcase appeared through the baggage flap. She heaved it on to the trolley. Two glass doors slid back before her. She passed from the cool silence of the terminal into a circus of heat. The crowd seemed to surge forward leaving in its wake one small man wearing a fixedly hopeful smile and holding up a white placard which read 'Hotel Riopuerte'. She was the only passenger from the airport bound for the hotel. He drove her there in a small, upholstered mini-bus. Sitting in it was like being inside a felted egg. They fled through the hot, blue streets.

The hotel on a busy thoroughfare overlooking the bay was like a cross between the bus and the terminal – cool and white on the outside, warm and heavy inside. Underneath the awning at the entrance a crowd was gathered. Hawkers and shoe-shine boys, some of them no more than children, arms outstretched to make that first, clamouring, almost sacred, contact. Some of them had thick ropes of gaudy beads strung around their arms or held up spangled T-shirts as if they were items of great delicacy. There were sores on their fingers; their smiles were like hideous gashes in the night. Judith passed through them on a wave of guilt-ridden coldness. After checking in, she was shown to her room. She ran a shower, leaving behind a trail of discarded, grimy clothes. It was always like a fresh start, the first shower in a strange city, an old skin sloughed off and swirling with the suds at her feet. She tumbled into bed, falling asleep to the soft lapping of the pool below and the tinkle of glasses rising up in the night.

She met Pacheas that first morning. (He would remind her of this afterwards although she had no clear memory of it.) Breakfast was served on the patio by the pool. The waiters were dressed smartly in white jackets with blue epaulettes which gave them a slightly military air. He was handsome. But weren't they all? Was it, she wondered, their reward for being poor. He carried himself as if he were on the precipice of his last breath. He was deferential but in a way which gave the impression that to serve was part of some great and noble tradition. And yet, she also felt he was mocking her. The way he swooped with plates or swatted away crumbs; all those waiterly flourishes, she distrusted them.

She sat eating sweetmeats and drinking bitter, black coffee and watched her counterparts, other European women, as they slithered like pale, wriggling fish into the pool with yelps of arch laughter. They paddled in the water as aimlessly as children, splashing one another with exaggerated glee. In the evenings they would be whisked off in a bus to a nightclub where they would whoop loudly through the night and end up singing raucously or slumped in the laps of their husbands. Judith watched them with a mixture of fascination and contempt.

It was on her fifth day in the city that Pacheas approached her. He stood over the table one morning without the
tray or the usual flourishes. A shadow fell over the map
she was studying. She had been planning to take a bus up
country into the dusty, underdeveloped parts where, she
had been told, people still lived as peasants. There in the
white glare of the hotel the very word 'peasant' seemed
absurd.

'It's a shame that you are always alone,' he said.

She looked up over the rims of her sunglasses, shocked
and surprised. Shock for the swift change from his half-
mocking manner of service – the breaking of the contract
– and surprise that he had spoken.

'It doesn't bother me, really.'

'If you wished for company . . . '

Aha, she thought, so that's what he's after.

'I'm Pacheas,' he said extending his hand. His palm
was pale and deeply creased. She touched his fingers
fleetingly.

'You have very good English, Pacheas.'

'I have been to the university.' He spoke in an almost
courtly fashion.

'I was studying . . . but the war, the revolution . . .
you understand.'

She didn't understand, really. She had seen the battle-
scarred streets of the old town. There were tattered flags
and banners still hanging from the porticoes and drapes
across balconies with great black exclamations on them,

or sometimes a clenched fist. On gable walls, once loud murals faded away into muteness under the sun's unflinching gaze. There were rubble-strewn gaps in the streets. Stray bricks nestled in the dry gutters. Sometimes Judith imagined she could get the faint whiff of something charred still smouldering away quietly. But the politics of it were beyond her. She found she had developed a wilful immunity to the low-lying misery around her. And yet, when she looked into Pacheas's eyes that morning she saw for an instant a core of hunger there that she couldn't ignore. It was like looking at pictures of starving refugees. There was a kind of hollow, innocent blamefulness there that tugged at her heart and made her feel both guilty and powerless, a seductive combination. She abandoned her wariness.

'Well, I was thinking of going to Santa Caterina today. I believe the monastery there is well worth seeing. Do you know it?'

'Yes,' he said, smiling triumphantly. 'I know it well. Today I am free. We could go together, yes?'

So it was arranged. They drove recklessly through the countryside creating rolling banks of dust that left high-tide marks on the windows of the car which Pacheas had borrowed from a friend for the day. It wheezed and rattled on the rough, red, rock-strewn roads. They reached Santa Caterina by noon, rambling through the shaded cloisters to escape the midday heat. A bell clanked overhead. In the quadrangle there was an orange tree laden down with fruit. They drank coconut milk at a street stall in the town and watched skinny, brown boys diving into the muddy river, leaping and arching like performing fish, for coins thrown in by a group of tourists on the bridge. Later, Pacheas drove back to San Quistador and took her around the city, through the slums and into the red-light district where as soon as dusk fell – as suddenly as if a curtain of deep, blue velvet had been drawn across the sky – little girls appeared and perched themselves on the bonnets of cars, their dirty, bony little knees drawn up to their stained chins, showing off their hairless pubes.

'So young!' Judith murmured.

'It is to prove that they are not what you call, soiled merchandise, yes?' he said brightly.

Through the open window Judith caught the stench of rotting fruit. They passed through the markets, through streets littered with wooden crates and the brown leaves of vegetables. Finally, Pacheas drove her down a narrow alley and into a cobbled courtyard surrounded on all sides by tall, dark, tenement buildings. She felt a sudden pang of fear. From an open window high above them pop music bleated plaintively. I will remember this, she thought to herself, the moment before violation. Pacheas got out and throwing his head back shouted up into the night sky. A face appeared at a window; a man grinned and waved. He will do nothing, Judith thought, they're in this together.

'My friend,' Pacheas explained. 'He owns the car.'

They walked back to the hotel, stopping on the way

for a meal at a little restaurant. A waiter fluttered around them.

'A busman's holiday,' Judith said, laughing. Pacheas didn't understand.

Naturally, they became intimate. She could almost hear Pacheas saying it in his stilted English. They had fallen into bed with a disturbing nonchalance yet he was a kind and passionate lover, often pausing to ask 'do I hurt?' as if she were a small, wounded animal. If he murmured to her it was always in English. His courtesy knew no bounds. There were none of Malcolm's breathless intimacies, none of his high-pitched urgency. Sometimes they lay there for hours enervated by the white heat of the afternoons but restful in the pool of their own silence. Yet each of them was aware of the passing of time. Judith crossed off each day in her diary, savouring their time together precisely because she knew it wouldn't last. What gave her a heavy heart was the prospect of going back to Malcolm. It struck her that she had barely thought of him these past weeks.

It was two days before she was due to leave that Pacheas mentioned marriage.

'I need a wife,' he said quietly one night as they lay together, the damp sheets crumpled around their knees.

Judith sat up, startled.

'What do you mean, you *need* a wife?'

'To get out. To get out, I need a wife. They would allow me to leave if I married an alien.'

The word alien winged its way around the room and landed again in their laps. She felt as if she were trapped in a blind alleyway with the sound of approaching footsteps.

'Is this what all this has been for?' She gestured to his prone body as if it too had had a part in the conspiracy.

He turned on his side away from her.

'Of course, I want to be with you, but with Malcolm . . . it is impossible.'

She wished she had never mentioned Malcolm.

'If I married you, at least I could be free. I could take up my studies again, get out of this hell.'

An image of his native village, the dusty township he had talked of, rose before her – his grandmother, black-shawled, leading the animals to water, his tubercular mother ailing in the American mission hospital, his brother, the rebel priest. It had never occurred to her that it might not be all he would want.

'It could be a marriage of convenience,' he said, 'isn't that what you call it?'

She let the idea settle. For almost a month she had feasted on poverty, poverty obligingly wearing parakeet colours, dressing up then stripping off, demanding nothing more than a glazed eye and a stray coin or two. Here was a chance to repay, to rid herself of the burden of feeling in some way beholden.

'No strings,' she said.

'Strings?'

'It would be a strictly business arrangement.'

He turned over and smiled broadly at her.

'Unless, Madame would wish it otherwise.'

My mistress treats me badly and for no reason. I know, of course, there is another man in her life who also calls her mistress. The word makes her agitated. She sweeps her hand angrily through her lush hair and there are bright tears in her eyes.

'That's all I'll ever be,' she says to Malcolm, 'your mistress.'

It doesn't upset her that she is my mistress. But then, ours is a very different relationship. I have no wife and family to go panting back to. I am faithful, dependent and despised. I remember when we were first together how she would speak to me. Sharing her secret fears with me, mainly about him, the swine! I have not much facility with language, or should I say expression, so I was a good listener. In the beginning when we came here, she and I would breakfast together on the balcony because she knew I loved the morning sun and missed the heat of home. It reminded me of our wedding breakfast. We went to the town hall in Santa Caterina early in the morning. We roused the mayor from his bed. Judith was wearing the white cotton dress she always wore by the pool. She looked so frail, as if the mounting heat might break her in two. The mayor, still rubbing sleep from his eyes, read from his book, and I translated for her. She took her vows in English. Afterwards we went back to the hotel. I changed into my uniform. She sat at her usual table and I served her. Who would have guessed, apart from our secretive, tender glances, that we were man and wife?

How can I explain my love for Judith? She would not have been the first white woman to stay in the Riopuerte that I had lusted after. No. But Judith was different. Her aloneness, firstly. Her fragile aloofness. Her generosity that day when I approached her nervously. Most other women would have treated me as just another randy – is that the word? – waiter, out for a conquest. But Judith was, how shall I put it, respectful. Or is it gracious? Yes, gracious. For that alone, I would forgive much.

I knew from the start that I had the key to her cool ardour. Malcolm, poor besotted Malcolm, doesn't. He rushes into the flat, flinging his coat on a chair, before reaching out and grasping her, smothering her in his hungry embrace. I have seen her flinch when he comes at her like that, baring teeth at his prey. Once he had her on the kitchen floor. He lay there, panting; their underclothes scattered on the tiles. How can she bear this indignity? Married men only lead to heartbreak, I've heard her say, but she continues to play his rough-and-tumble game. He plays other games too, games of make-believe. 'If only,' he says, 'if only . . .'

Of course, Malcolm doesn't realise my significance in the household. Judith has told him I'm a student staying in the box room until my permit comes through. He was wary at first, jealous even (how dare *he* be jealous!), suspecting I was some kind of 'live-in lover', as he put it. But Judith reassured him.

'Malcolm, he barely has a word of English,' she told him impatiently. Strangely, this satisfied him. Fool! Believing that words are a prerequisite for love. That moment when she lied for me I felt a hopeless tremor in my heart as if the old conspiracy between us had been rekindled. But it came to nothing. Malcolm need have no fears. Her loyalty is slavish. Since we've reached these colder climes I have not been in her bed. After such tenderness I have known only coldness. When Malcolm is not here I sometimes stand hidden by her doorway and watch her while she sleeps. Oh, the careless thrust of her arm across the bed, her fingers entwined in her treacle-coloured hair! And then to see her rise. Her artless beauty, the little knobs of her spine, the shadows between her shoulder blades. These things that were mine, all mine.

Lately, though, her coolness has turned into something more sinister. She wants to be rid of me. She asks why I am not arranging for my studies and warns that I cannot live with her forever – oh, but I could, Judith, I could! I cannot tell her now that I have lied to her. That I dropped out of university; that I learned my English from women like her at the Riopuerte; that my mother is hale and hearty and running a brothel in Estanza; that I have no brother; that I could have left Quistador any time I wanted. She would never have married me had she known these things. Oh no! My fair Judith wanted a holiday romance. If I had declared my love she would have despised me then, and I would have never captured her. No, I had to appear selfish and grasping before I could do that. A strange way indeed to win someone over . . .

During the day I wander around her flat. It is a cold place, purpose-built, with straight, regular rooms. It looks as if she furnished it from a catalogue or went around the store blindfolded picking things at random. They are all tasteful items in themselves but they sit awkwardly with one another. Like Judith and I. And yet, I have grown used to my caged existence. In three months' time our marriage will be recognised here but in the meantime I must lie low and not draw attention to myself in any way. I tell myself that I am lucky to live in the same orbit as the one I love. But like the plant she brought back from Quistador which wilts now on the bathroom windowsill, its flaming leaves paled by too much Northern light, I too am ailing from neglect. I sometimes fear that Judith will never recognise my love and that in the end I shall have to force it on her. I am, after all, her husband.

TWO CHINA DOGS

BY PITY AND CONTEMPT I have learned. Pity, mostly, in the moist eyes of women, in their tender touches. They seek out my mark and kiss it as passionately as if it were a relic – the chipped hip bone of a saint, the pickled tongue of a martyr. Afterwards they dress quickly and wave shyly before leaving, hugging their secret compassion to themselves. Relief leaves the hospital ward. One-night stands. No time for them to creak open the shallow boats of *their* hearts to reveal the soft pulp of cockle, thank God. They use words like 'gentle' to describe me, a euphemism for ineffectual, I suspect, but what of it? You are my woman for tonight. Cradle me in your arms and I shall tell you all . . .

Let us go back to that vital moment in my life, the moment of conception, where perhaps all our motifs are set. Picture this. A fairground. Bright bobbins of light unfurling themselves into the night sky. Tinny music playing, the air rent with screaming. In a dark field behind the biggest tent a wet flap of canvas slaps against two prone bodies. Cold wet blades of grass brush against my mother's cheek. He enters her in one rough, urgent thrust. She looks up at the inky sky and sees in the pale, brooding clouds only monsters, cloaked figures limping horribly, their gnarled faces turned away eclipsed by the twitch of a hood. Two china dogs sit in the dewy grass. Snub-nosed, speckled, black-and-white creatures gazing absently at my mother's clenched, averted face, my father's craggy hand. She has won them at the coconut shy.

They married. Jack left his beloved fairground and settled in Reginald Street. Two pockmarked terraces sewn into the underside of the city's skirts, each door showing a bright ruddy face to the street. All the usual preparations were made. A baby carriage was bought. A high-sprung purple carriage on huge spoked wheels. A satin-hearted holy picture hung from the hood – the first cloud on my horizon. Jack, holding me in his ungainly arms, said the mark might disappear. My mother vaguely tried to justify the random hand of God.

'It was an accident,' she told me when I was still small, 'a fight among the angels and the red dye got spilt, that's all.'

Oh, it's an ugly thing. A liver-coloured stain covering the left side of my face, trickles of it right down as far as my collar-bone and a stray splash over my eyebrow. A rather grand aunt of mine – on my mother's side – called it the port wine stain. Made me feel like a tablecloth soiled at a society party. Jack was wrong. It grew as I grew. The worst of it is that it comes on people suddenly. If I had a gammy leg they would have some warning. They would hear my irregular footsteps approaching, the villain with the lame walk.

A sunny nature might have compensated, but I was a sullen child. I would sit in the playpen, the toys ranged carefully outside, staring solemnly through the bars. I remember the strange distortions of my caged world. Huge legs and feet, my mother's mottled calves, the glint of her copper hair as she bent to pick me up, her eyes the startled green of an angry cat's bearing down on me. She complained that I made strange with people. But it was *they* who made strange with me. Neighbours would not bend over cooing into this pram, or if they did, they would suddenly withdraw, uncertain and embarrassed. After a while my mother stopped leaving the pram out in the cool shade of the street as was the custom. My world began to shrink.

Inside our house was a catalogue of the unwanted and the cherished side-by-side. At either end of our parlour mantelpiece sat the two china dogs; there was a broken clock frozen at five past eight like the poignant memento of some tragedy (my birth, perhaps?), their wedding photo, stray pennies, a luminous statue of the Virgin Mary and a barometer on a wooden plaque that always registered cloudy. Here, away from the prying eyes of the street, my mother devised games for me. Hide-and-seek.

'At the count of ten I'll come looking for you,' she would call out from the scullery.

Silence fell over the house. She would stalk through the rooms calling my name with a threatening kind of tenderness.

'Bernard, Bernard . . . '

Sometimes, though, she would retreat quietly to the kitchen leaving me alone, cramped in a cupboard or some other dark place sweating with fearful anticipation.

Her conversations were full of a yearning for brutality. 'There was a girl in Barrett Street, mental, you know, who was locked in the back room for thirty years, her food shoved into her on a plate,' she told me with grim relish. 'Then her mother died and they came to get her. She was like some wild thing, her hair all matted. They had to strap her down. And when she was brought out the daylight nearly blinded her . . . '

I sometimes longed myself for a dark room, someone at whom I could bare my teeth, instead of the perilous version of normality she offered me.

As for Jack, that wrinkled blur in my memory, Jack loved anything that deflected attention from himself. He worked as a handyman, the sort of man who appeared cheerily at back doors of houses and 'fixed' things while women grumbled to him about their husbands. I doubt if anyone on that street remembers him now, or if they do, it would only be as a twisted, truncated body under a sink or as a pair of stout legs up a ladder. He was born in a caravan just as a fireworks display burst upon the night to celebrate the end of the war. He had had a colourful, ragged childhood. When he talked about it, it was as if a hundred gaudy lights switched on in his head.

'In my day the side-shows were the thing. They didn't come just for the rides, they came to see the freaks. They used to sit in little booths down the middle of the fair and you paid a penny for a peep.'

'Jack, please . . . ' my mother would say casting anxious glances in my direction.

But he would go on regardless. There was The Fat Lady, weighing forty stone; The China Doll, a perfectly formed midget who, for a price, would sit like a piece of icing on grown men's laps; The Leopard Man, whose skin was covered with great brown moles from which tufts of hair sprang and the Two-Headed Monster, a pair of coal-black twins joined at the hip and shoulder and sharing, it was reputed, the one heart – these were the creatures my mother saw that night.

I envied the sense of celebration that surrounded them. When I stepped out on to the street, I met only silence, the world retreating in bafflement. A football idling at the kerb, goalpost jumpers like cowpats, abandoned, a slate stranded on a hopscotch square. No one would pay money to gawp at me.

There were other humiliations, too. The spring before my father died a hand gently tapped on the door of Number 9. I opened it to find a gaggle of girls outside, a wave of nervous laughter woven into a tapestry of girlish limbs. One of them, Sadie Corcoran from

Balfe Street, I remember, landed a big wet kiss on my cheek.

'There,' she said turning triumphantly to her companions. 'I told you I could do it.'

My mother spat the word Judas after her but I did not feel so betrayed. It was my first kiss, after all.

Jack died on a pallid summer's evening the day after my fifteenth birthday. He was mowing the Green, a large square of grass in front of the monastery. Brother Stanislaus looked out of the schoolhouse window in time to see the white flail of his dimpled arm as he fell silently in a crumpled heap on the scorched stubble. Two nuns from the convent came to lay him out. The dark brown habit, his rigid jaw, the yellowed skin and the pennies stuck in the hollows of his eyes to keep the lids closed were like Jack's last attempt at a macabre, self-effacing joke.

That was when I first met Madge and Bernie. Madge was my father's sister, big like him, with great misshapen breasts, wads of fat around her middle and two chins. She stood on our doorstep and wept. I had never seen such abundant tears. My mother steered her into the house, gave her a cup of tea and let her sob away. Bernie hung back. When she was finally persuaded in she sat on a kitchen chair swinging her legs. She was a rough-looking girl about my own age. She had stringy brown hair which fell into her eyes in a spiky fringe. Her hands were wizened at the knuckles. She picked her nose absently. When Madge was taken upstairs to view the corpse we were left alone in the kitchen. From above we heard another agonised howl, a prelude to a fresh bout of weeping. Bernie threw her eyes heavenward. We giggled.

'I wish we could stay for the funeral but . . . Jack would have understood,' Madge said as they were leaving.

'Of course,' my mother said, 'the show must go on.'

'But if there's anything you need you've only got to say the word. We'd take the boy for you. Do him good to knock around with us for a summer.'

She turned and beamed at me. 'Sure he has it in his blood.'

These words must have sent a chill down my mother's spine. Or perhaps she was glad that they had come to claim me back. For whatever dark reason she decided to take them up on the offer. Madge met me at the station and carried me off to the fairground in a smelly, rattling van. Bernie crouched in the back. They were camped in a field near the sea. A sharp, tangy breeze came in over the dunes. The name 'Halpin' – my name – was emblazoned on a fluttering banner across the entrance. We tramped through the grass, soon to be bludgeoned by a thousand footfalls. It was early morning, the sky was a smock of timid blue. Men were about putting up tents and rides. It was just as Jack had described. The big wheel, the chair-o-planes lashed together, dodgems snoozing in a bunch like a litter of puppies, gay, frozen horses on the merry-go-round. But where were the booths?

'Oh, that stuff, that's all gone now,' Madge said disparagingly. 'People go for the mechanical things now – more fun.'

I wondered where all those monsters had gone. Were they closeted in back rooms or just living in quiet, baffled streets like mine? Shame, I thought, we could have compared notes.

That first night I stayed with Madge and Bernie in their caravan. As soon as the lights went out and Madge had heaved over into her first bout of sleep, I heard a shifting from the top bunk and saw Bernie's legs climb down, her rubbed-looking shift riding up over her pale bottom.

'Are you awake, Bernard?' she whispered to me in the darkness. 'I have something to show you. Want to see?'

I thought for a moment that maybe she had a birthmark hidden away somewhere. But no. She lifted up her nightie. I caught a glimpse of breast, pale as moonlight, her thin, startled-looking ribs, a tuft of brown hair between her legs. I reached out to touch her but she drew back.

'No, no,' she said, 'you only get to look.'

They were garish summers. They pass before my eyes, a bright ticker-tape of colour. I came to know each creaking board on the rides. I started on the dodgems, large droning insects with flickering antennae. I watched the people wheeling and juddering around like drunken waltzers, gagging with the most delicious fear.

This was no involuntary recoiling; they had come to be terrified and my hand on the quaking lever decided when it would stop. At last, *I* had control. But the dodgems were only kids' stuff. I moved on to the roller coaster where the high shrieks of children would tear your eardrums apart. I looked into the silent, gaping holes of their frightened laughter. The ghost train was the best. I sent whole carriage loads of them away into the rumbling darkness. Inside, soft monsters were afoot, brushing up against damp cheeks. Spiders, too, and bats, swooped low and midway through the ride, a giant flash lit up the hollow eyes and cackling jaws of skeletons on the creeping walls of canvas. Hearts pounding they went home to quiet rooms, dark streets, their own secrets. And, after each summer, I went home there as well . . .

Nothing changes in Reginald Street. Its menacing familiarity remains intact. When I go back there to see my mother I walk into a mirror that has reversed. It is she who is huddled in a dark corner of the parlour now, rocking herself gently to sleep in the gloomy afternoons. She will not look me in the eye. For her – as for others – my face is a dark booth. Once inside, as in moving clouds, they choose pictures to haunt themselves with. For her, the stain of unshed menstrual blood, perhaps. I have learned the power of imperfection. Others hide their flaws deep down and offer them as prizes for intimacy, while mine is here, right here, up front. Enter, at your peril. Like my mother's china dogs, I watch from inside a hollowed-out shell, quite cold and perfect.

DIVIDED
ATTENTION

HE RANG FIRST three months ago – at three in the morning. The phone blundered into my fogged brain and I lay in bed not sure if the burring was in my ears or the vestige of a dream phone. But then, phones in dreams ring, don't they? They're usually the old, black, bakelite models – as if the fixtures of our dreams are awaiting modernisation. It continued for several minutes, not a demon of sleep but a whimpering child waiting to be picked up. Alarmed, I padded to the kitchen. It could only be death at this hour, death or bad news, or . . . you. I shook the thought away. I was no longer a woman waiting for the phone to ring. I lifted the receiver.

'Hello?'

Silence.

'Hello?' I heard my own puzzled tone echo back at me. Still nothing.

'Hello?' Mild aggravation now – I know that tone from the receiving end. 'Who is this?'

The silence persisted. Why is it so disconcerting on the phone. Why does it yawn so? Minutes gape.

'Hello!'

There was a shifting sound. I got the impression of

a large bulk wedged into a small space. Then an exerted
breathing. It was laboured, distressed even. Was someone
hurt, wounded in some way? I conjured up pictures of a
street fight, or a mugging, a man stumbling into a phone
box clutching a bloody side and dialling the first number
that came into his head. Was it someone I knew? Victor,
I thought. A friend of mine, an asthmatic with a comic
book name, prone to late night, melancholy drinking. You
wouldn't know him. When he is distressed he makes this
gnawing sound, a device he uses to reassure himself that
he will draw the next lungful.

'Victor, is that you, Victor?'

The breathing intensified, louder now, more protesting.

'Are you all right, Victor? Are you hurt? What's wrong?'

There was a harrumphing noise like a horse snorting
and the breathing shifted up a gear, quicker, more jagged. I heard in it a rising panic, an urgency that had
not been there before. And then, only then, I realised.
This was an obscene call. I slammed the receiver down.
I was shaking. The phone sat there, implacable. Flat as
a pancake, the little square buttons in their serried rows,
the receiver safely in its snug depressions, the letter-box
window stoutly declaring my number, the coy curl of
its flex. How often had I sat staring at it, willing it to
ring, cursing it for its refusal. But then it had been a
co-conspirator, imbued with a delicious imminence as if
it too was longing to hear from you. It was traitorous
sometimes, but never *this*, never spiteful. Now it had

invited a pervert into my home. How could I ever trust it again?

You would have said, change your number, that's what you would have said. I know exactly the tone you would use – emphatic, overlaid with a professional concern. You managed that combination well. A sort of alms-giving affection. Go ex-directory, you would have said, like me. What a relief, you once said, no more crank calls. Precisely! You didn't know I had your number, did you? I got it by stealth. Oh, I looked in the directory hoping to find your name there carelessly among imposters. There are five who share your name in the book, all of whom could have been you but none of them were. I pitied those who were not you, I pitied anyone who thought one of these frauds was you. But that was early on. It was only later that I pitied myself.

It started innocently, I swear. I had not intended ever to use your number. Having it alone was enough. I carried it around in my wallet, taking it out from time to time and contemplating it, wondering what it would be like for this particular conjunction of figures to be familiar – oh, let's not beat around the bush – to be *mine*. I wanted them to spell out home. It soothed me to have it; it was connection, that was all, just connection. And it served as my lucky charm, like a rabbit's foot, which had the power to conjure you up and granted me an ownership which you knew nothing about. As long as I had your number, I would be safe.

Celia told me to report the call.

'You must protect yourself,' she said. Her stout face flushed angrily, her perm bounced. 'The bastard!'

Much like what she said of you.

You once remarked that she had the sort of looks that would have won a bonny baby competition. Ruddy cheeks, plump arms, a stolid, ready smile, those curls. Can't you see her in bonnet and pantaloons, you said. Watch the birdie, Celia! I used to smile when I saw her and remembered that, a sly, complicitous smile, a smile for *you*. It was part of our language, the secret, mocking language of lovers. Now I look at Celia squarely in the face and think – she is here; you are not.

I didn't report it. I don't know why. Laziness, perhaps, embarrassment. But no, it was more than that. I was resisting this man, and his method of entry into my life. I didn't want him to force me into changing my number. I didn't want him to have the power to make me fear my own telephone. I didn't want the notion of him to make any difference to me – echoes, echoes. And anyway, I couldn't bring myself to describe the call. If I put it into words, it would sound flat and neutral. What was it but a series of silences punctuated by heaving and gasping? Who would understand the great gap between what it was and how it made me feel? Perhaps it *had* been

Victor. He would ring soon and say shamefacedly 'look, about the other night . . . '

But my biggest fear was that the policeman logging the call down in the large ledger of misdemeanours would look up at me and know that I too have been a caller in my time.

I rang your number first as an experiment, simply to see if I could. And I was curious too, about your other life. The Wife, the Two Daughters, the Baby. *She* answered.

'809682, hello?'

I heard the sun in her voice; it spoke to me of gaiety and ease. I saw a blonde woman, hair scraped back in a workaday ponytail (that you might later loosen), a floral dress, bare legs and sandals. She was slightly out of breath as if she had run in from the garden. In the background a child was wailing. She said 'excuse me' and put her hand over the mouthpiece.

'Emily,' I heard her say, 'give Rachel the teddy. You must learn to share.'

'Hello?' she said again slightly crossly.

I put the phone down swiftly.

Of course, it didn't stop there. Curiosity knows no boundaries. The first call had rewarded me with your daughters' names – you had always referred to them as The Children, an anonymous troop of foot soldiers. But then, I suppose, my name was never uttered in your household.

I picked times when I knew you wouldn't be there.

You see, it was not you I wanted, but your world. Sometimes, Emily – or was it Rachel? – answered. They would deliver your number in a piping voice before the receiver was taken away. I got to know the sounds of your house. Your doorbell has chimes. Your hallway has no carpet – I have heard the tinny crash of toys falling on a hard surface. The television is in a room close to the phone. I have heard its muffled explosions, the clatter and boom of cartoons before your wife says: 'Emily, *please* shut the door.'

He rang again. Same time. He's a creature of habit. This time I was awake. I had come in from a party – yes, I'm getting out now, mixing, meeting people. I was making coffee. There was a vague drumming in my temples that would later become a hangover. I was still in my finery, or some of it. I had kicked off my shoes and was removing my earrings when the phone trilled. I lifted it and knew immediately it was him. The quality of *his* silence is different; it is the silence of ambush. This time I said nothing, remembering with shame my response the first time, my babbling concern for Victor which had exposed me as a stupid woman who didn't recognise an obscene call even in the middle of it. I thought too that if I said nothing, *he* would be forced to speak.

As time went by, I got more adventurous, or desperate. I rang once at three a.m. – the witching hour! Nothing malicious, I promise; I simply wanted to hear your voice. You answered almost immediately. There must be another phone by the bed. You must have been awake. Perhaps you had just made love to her and you were having a cigarette, resting the ash-tray on your chest and blowing smoke rings into the air, your arm lazily around her shoulder. *This*, I know.

'Hello?' you said.

'Larry,' I heard her whisper, 'who is it?'

Larry, she calls you Larry.

And then, there was another sound. The gurgling of a baby, the drowsy, drugged stirrings of a child suckling. The night feed.

'Don't know,' I heard you say thoughtfully.

Was that suspicion in your voice?

I imagined you withdrawing your arm from around her.

'Just a wrong number,' I heard you say before the line went dead.

They say that you should laugh at flashers. Cuts them down to size, literally. But with a caller, my caller, it was more difficult. He operated on my imagination. I wondered what he did in the phone-box. (I always thought of him in a phone-box though he could have been ringing from the comfort of his own home.) I imagined him fumbling with his fly as I answered, then rubbing himself, abandoning himself to his own grim joy while I listened. He wanted me – anyone – to listen. And what did he get out of it? Horror, fear, abuse maybe. Perhaps that's what drove him on. That was another thing; he never reached a climax. Maybe he couldn't and that was his problem. Or maybe my silence, my intent listening inhibited him.

I remember once hearing my mother make love. She had been out and came home late. I heard the scrape of the key in the lock and the sound of coarse whispering in the hall. The stairs creaked. The loose floorboard on the landing, which I knew how to avoid, groaned. My mother giggled. I imagined her leading someone by the hand, a blind man not familiar with the obstacles of our house – the low chest on the landing, the laundry basket that held the bathroom door ajar. He stumbled against something.

'Ssh,' she urged, 'the children!'

I lay, stiff with wakefulness, as they went into her room. A thin wall separated us. In the darkness I manufactured pictures. A skirmish in a cobbled square, her bed a high-sprung carriage rocked by a baying crowd. A cry! My mother's, sharp and high. Has someone hurled a stone? The crowd sets to with more vigour, heaving, pushing. She cries again but it is muffled as if she is being thrown against the coach's soft upholstery. I hear the tramp of boots on oily cobbles – left, right, left, right – the icy whip of bayonets, the vicious sheen of blades. A groan. He staggers; she cries out 'no!' I hammer with my fists against the wall. Stop, stop!

I rang the night of the party. New Year. Tradition,

you said, we always have a crowd in. You looked at me ruefully.

'I'd much prefer to be with you, you know that.' You shrugged.

I called close to midnight. A guest answered. I felt safe to speak your name.

'Hold on,' she said gaily, 'I'll get Laurence. Laurence . . . it's for you.'

The receiver was put down. For several minutes I was a gatecrasher at your party. Oh, how festive it sounded! There was a noisy crescendo of conversation, the ring of laughter, a male voice above the din calling plaintively 'the opener, has anyone seen the bottle opener?'

I saw plates of steaming food being handed across a crowded room, glasses foaming at the rim, streamers trailing from your hair.

'Hello!' you cried triumphantly – several drinks on. 'Excuse the noise. Party!'

I could have spoken then but I didn't. What would I have said? Happy New Year from a wellwisher. No, then you would have known the power I had over you, the power to betray *you*.

'Oops,' I heard a woman cry, 'careful!'

I didn't, of course, betray you. But knowing that I could changed things. I had to stop ringing for fear I would blurt it out – our secret. The snatched moments, the meetings in pubs, the subterfuge. Instead, I have to admit it, I went to your house. Just once. Once was enough.

It was at night. I took the train. I crossed the metal bridge at your station imagining your gaze on its familiar struts. The stationmaster snoozed in his booth, his chin resting on his soiled uniform. He didn't check my ticket. This made me feel invisible, convinced me that I wasn't really doing this – making a pilgrimage to the shrine of your home. You see, even at the height of what I felt for you I realised how foolish I'd become. As I trod down the leafy passage leading from the station I heard the singing of the rails as another train approached, the train my sensible self would have boarded for the city. But it pulled away without her; there was no going back now. I picked my way through the quiet, darkening streets. It was late spring, fragrant after rain. Petals floated in the kerbside puddles. A fresh breeze soughed in the trees. I passed the lighted windows of other homes. Their warm, rosy rooms were on display. Sometimes I glimpsed a family tableau. A father in an armchair, one child on his lap, another perched on the armrest. A granny with a walking frame and sagging face – a stroke victim, I guessed – being hauled to her feet by a young woman plump with goodness. Two blonde girls sitting cross-legged on a window seat plaiting one another's hair.

You live on a high, sloping avenue overlooking the bay. The lights of the city jostled on the skyline, beacons flooding the water with silent messages, mouthing like goldfish. I approached your house like a thief, with darting looks up and down the street. I cringed at the creak of the gate, slipping quickly around it to hide behind the large oak, the only tree in the garden. I leaned gratefully against its bark. There was a muddied bare patch at its base as if it had sheltered others before me and I knew I would find hearts and arrows carved on its trunk. Your house stands on its own. Pleasing, symmetrical, five windows around an arched doorway. It was ablaze with light. I must have stood there for hours growing chilled and stiff as the night closed in, the sky turning to indigo. The swift stealth of the moon threw the garden into relief.

I was rewarded – finally. The front door opened. An orange beam of light flooded down the path. I peered from my fronds of shadow. And then your voice.

' . . . and then it's straight to bed!'

You were holding the hand of a dark-haired child of about five. Rachel, or at least I decided it was Rachel.

'Amn't I a good girl, Daddy, amn't I?'

'Yes, of course you are.'

'Am I your favourite?'

A dog bounded down the garden. I froze. You never told me you had a dog. He frisked on the lawn and Rachel whooped delightedly.

'Look, Daddy, look at Brandy!' (Brandy – what a name for a dog. Why didn't you go the whole hog and call it Smirnoff?) Brandy trailed towards the gate.

'Brandy, Brandy,' you called.

I stiffened, fearing the dog would smell the stranger in your midst and would expose me, panting victoriously at my feet. I imagined you finding me there, cowering in the undergrowth. How could I explain? There was no explanation except that I wanted to see you. I held my breath, terrified. You were close now. I could smell *you*, but it seemed that I had stood there for so long that my odour of fear and longing had been taken up by the very veins of the leaves and belonged now to the garden itself. Rachel saved me.

'Daddy,' she wailed. 'Daddy, where are you? I can't see you.'

'It's all right, darling, I'm here.'

'Daddy?'

'It's okay.' You halted, a hair's breadth away. 'I'm still here.'

You turned away and walked into a sudden shaft of moonlight. Seeing you thus, I ached to be discovered, to share in the tenderness you saved for this little girl. The dog scampered up the path ahead of you. Rachel rushed out of the gloom and clung to your waist. You lifted her up and carried her inside drawing the train of light in after you. The door closed.

I was alone, shut out where I belonged, in the pit of the garden.

I've told all this to my caller. I've named him Larry in your honour. I've had to battle against his groaning and heaving but I've persisted. He keeps ringing so it must do something for him. It's therapy for me, you could say. Therapy, indeed! I can see you wrinkle your nose disdainfully. I needed to tell someone. I needed to tell *you* – but he's a good second best. I address the noisy static that is his frustration. I am happier that he is preoccupied – as you were in your way – and that he is not listening exclusively to me. I could not bear undivided attention.

Last week I threw your number away. The paper on which it was written was yellowed and grubby and ragged along the folds. The ink had almost faded away. I found it had lost its power. Does this mean I'm cured? Of you, perhaps.

PLAQUE

HER TEETH MUST have been rotting quietly for months but she only discovered this the morning after Jimmy left. She was sitting in the kitchen, alone and eerily calm. Everything around her had suddenly become more angular. The edges of the table, the corners of the worktops, the angle of the open door seemed sharper, hostile somehow. She was chewing one of the child's toffees – he had left one on the table – the sullen round of mastication leading her into a kind of void where only the shrapnel of memories reached her . . .

Jimmy, blundering out of the bathroom one morning; he had cut himself while shaving and there was blood streaming from his upper lip. She was standing at the top of the stairs. It was like watching a wounded, trapped animal. He filled the narrow passageway, blocking out the light as he lumbered towards her, propelled by some unstoppable rage. And she thought, just for one moment, he's going to kill me. He lunged at her, catching a bunch of her dressing gown in his fist, blood trickling between his fingers, shouting in to her face, 'don't just stand there, *do* something . . . ' He was utterly repentant afterwards. He came home at lunch-time to apologise. An ugly scab had formed on his lip.

'It was nothing,' she had said. And so it was. But yet, she couldn't shift the idea from her mind that in the moment when he had stood over her like that, he *might* have killed her. And little random things he said and did from then on seemed a veiled way of telling her that he would eventually damage her. That other morning in the kitchen, little Jimmy whining into his cereal, she, desperately trying to quell a saucepan of boiling milk as it dropped hissing on the stove, the radio clamouring, he had said in a pursed mutter: 'This place is a madhouse.' She could hear both threat and blame in it. And that time in the garden when he was chopping wood, flailing the axe high in the air and turning to her at the window with a triumphant smile as the amputated log wobbled and reeled drunkenly away – even *that* was saying something. Yet on the surface of their lives all was calm . . .

Suddenly there was a small sucking sound followed by a cold blast on the left side of her mouth as if a windy gap had just opened up. She felt a hard bit of filling roll out on to her tongue. She extricated the toffee carefully and there it was, a molten piece of silver stuff embedded in the gnawed, sticky mess. She prized it free – it seemed important, somehow, to save it – and wrapped it in a piece of tissue paper. Maybe if she put it under her pillow, Jimmy might come back.

Damn it, her teeth were always letting her down. She had always wanted a perfectly even, white set of teeth and had got instead a dull band of yellow the colour of ageing piano keys. She wouldn't have minded if they had been slightly blemished by those bleached patches that a lack of calcium sometimes leaves, if they had only been white in the first place. She remembered her first date with Jimmy, his arm around her in the car, his finger stroking her chin.

'Can I ask you a question?'

She nodded.

'You won't be hurt now, will you?'

'No . . . ,' doubtfully.

'What happened to your teeth? I mean, the colour, were they *always* like that?'

Omens, she thought, omens.

The next minute there was a loud crash. She turned, startled, to see a young man with a hammer in his hand crouching on the windowsill and grinning madly at her. He must have shattered the window with just one lazy swing and the pane had fallen in large shards, some of them teetering on the sill, the others sliding, one by one, onto the draining board, each with a brazen clatter.

'Did I give you a fright?'

He stooped in through the empty frame, his heavy, metal-tipped boots grazing against the plates left draining on the rack.

'We thought we'd attack from the back . . . '

He was cheerful enough for an armed attacker, but shouldn't he be wearing a hood, or a balaclava or something? Afterwards – if there was one – she would be able to identify his bony wrists, his sandy hair. She caught sight of a steel ladder propped up behind him and another pair of overalled legs disappearing up it. So there was a couple of them in it.

'The boss is out front sorting out the gear. We tried the front door but there was no reply.'

Oh my God, she thought, the windows! It was the last thing she and Jimmy had agreed on. Aluminium windows, front and back. She couldn't stop them now. Already from upstairs she could hear the sound of breaking glass.

There were three of them. The boss was a small, rumpled man in his fifties with loose-fitting spectacles whose hinges had long since collapsed and were bound up with grubby sticking plaster. There was the sandy-haired fellow (the armed attacker she liked to call him to herself) and a darker, chubby boy who seemed to be the apprentice. She found their presence in the house both comforting and disturbing. They filled the house, yet made it seem paper-thin. She found it odd to sit in her own home with the legs, torsos and crotches of three strange men appearing at the windows, which were no longer windows but huge, gaping holes. It was like being inside one of those cut-away diagrams in a building manual which depicts houses as skeletons and solid walls as only cavities filled with wads of perforated stuff. She had to feed

them at regular intervals. They sprawled around the kitch-
en table, their long, loose, dusty limbs seeming cramped
in a room she had always considered . . . well, spacious.
They liked their tea strong and heavily sugared and they
smoked constantly. At lunch-time they opened up unruly
packages of batch-loaf sandwiches and ate voraciously.

'Doesn't your husband come home for lunch?' the
sandy-haired one asked.

'No, not any more.'

'Not worried about leaving you here all on your own?'
He grinned.

'Jimmy knows I can look after myself,' she said tartly,
taking up his tone.

She was pleased with this fabrication, and the tacit
assumption that her world was still somehow intact.
After an hour the men rose reluctantly from the table. As
she did the washing-up her fingers struck the soft pulp of
sugar left at the bottom of their cups which seemed like a
subversive residue of their jaunty mood.

The tooth was really nagging her now. Her tongue kept
on seeking out the cavity and the raw, tender part which
tingled with an oddly pleasant pain. She decided to ring the
dentist. The men were using a drill so there was an insistent
high-pitched whining coming from upstairs as she waited
for the receptionist to leaf through the appointment book.

'Well, Mrs Chambers, you're in luck. Dr Grimes has
a cancellation this afternoon – at three. If you're in pain,
I'm sure we could fit you in then.'

If you're in pain . . . the drill lurched on to a higher note. 'Thank you, that'll be fine,' she said.

It was only when she put the phone down that she remembered Jimmy, little Jimmy. Poor boy had been saddled with that 'little' bit for too long. From now on there would be no need for it. He would be home from school by then. Today, of all days, she should be at home. Today she must tell him. The sandy-haired youth passed as she sat pondering by the phone. 'Problems?'

She explained about the dental appointment.

'Ah, not to worry,' he said, venturing to touch her arm high up. 'Sure won't *we* keep an eye on the lad for you?'

'Would you? *Really?*'

'We'll explain to him. He won't make strange with us now, will he?'

Quite the opposite, she thought. He would be delighted with this invasion of men with their hammers, chisels and drills, their dusty boxes of nails and greasy pails of nuts and bolts. And no mother to warn him off. Bliss! She put on her coat and left a note for him. He was nearly eight, after all. As she left the house she felt quite exhilarated by the swift, sudden change in her routine and the recklessness of leaving behind a 'latchkey' child.

She had been going to the same dentist since she was a child. She was familiar with every hair of his white, brush-like moustache and the dark crypts of his nostrils, having been at close quarters with his porous lower face for years. This man was as familiar with her mouth as . . . as Jimmy was. But more than that, he had rearranged it, much as someone changes the look of a room by moving the furniture around. He had whipped out her milk teeth which had refused to fall, he had fixed braces and he had filled most of the teeth she now had. He was also the only person who actually liked her teeth.

'Not a great colour,' he had conceded, 'but, by God, they're strong!'

Incredible as it was to her, he enjoyed his work. He talked of it as if he were party to some vast struggle between good and evil, probing blindly in a livid, crimson world where teeth were like stones harbouring crawling colonies on their undersides.

'Hello, stranger,' he said as she was shown into the surgery. He looked at her chart.

'Trouble, I suppose.' He sighed.

'I've lost a filling.'

He motioned her to sit in the chair. From a gleaming tray of implements behind him he chose two – a thin, hooked one and a little mirror on a stem.

'Now, let's see . . . open . . . wider.'

The mirror lay coldly on her tongue. He touched the tooth almost immediately. She winced.

'Aha!' he said triumphantly.

She thought it would end at that but he continued to work his way around her mouth, scraping vigorously as he went.

'Mmn . . . ' He clicked his tongue. 'Well, young lady, that's the least of your problems.' How could *he* know?

He straightened, wagging a creased finger at her.

'These things don't come adrift for nothing.'

He laid the hook down.

'Looks like periodontitis.'

'What?'

'We may be able to save some of them.'

'But I haven't felt a thing.'

'These gum diseases are sneaky buggers, you know. They don't give much warning. Have your gums been bleeding much?'

'They were a few months back, but then it stopped.'

'Aha, well that's just it,' he said, warming to his subject. 'You see, it all starts off with plaque. Nasty thing, plaque. Sort of film. Clings to your teeth, then attacks the gums. That's when the bleeding starts. Then all goes quiet again.'

A baby yowled in the waiting-room.

'But that's when the real damage is being done, when the fibre holding tooth and gum together is being loosened, until gradually the tooth loses contact with its neighbour.'

He rose and went to a cabinet at the back of the room.

'Curious, really, but the gums stop bleeding at that stage and look pink and healthy again. And all that's left is an unpleasant taste in the mouth and a hint of bad breath.'

He came back with a needle in his hand. He was

usually clumsy with injections and they always hurt. She saw him lower the needle into her mouth as if watching him through a convex mirror, his huge, trembling hand sprouting from the pinhead of his face. He left her alone to allow the numbness to set in. She lay back, her head resting on the high, arched back of the chair, her legs splayed out in front of her, foreshortened by the angle. A great menacing bulb hung over her and at her elbow, water gently swirled in the white globe of a small basin. Behind her she could hear him making up a mixture to put in her tooth. He came back with it, a knob of pale putty on a glass disc.

'Now, how are we doing here?'

He stuck an ungainly finger into the thickened underside of her cheek. Then he sat down on his high stool, one foot resting on the rung as if he were at a bar.

'And how's that husband of yours?'

He was fiddling with the fitting for the drill, drawing it over on a pulley.

Well, actually, she rehearsed, he's just walked out. No, tomorrow, tomorrow she would start telling people, but today would be as numbed and sterile as her deadened cheek.

'He's fine, just fine.'

Dr Grimes took some of the flesh-coloured putty up in a hook and wedged it into the cavity. The drill started to whine, grinding softly into her jaw. It seemed she couldn't get away from the sound of drilling. Every so often he would pause and say 'rinse' and she would spit into the little basin beside her. Then he would hand her a glass of pink, oily stuff which she swilled around her mouth. It mixed strangely with that other gritty, metallic taste. She was sorry when the back-and-forth movement ceased because it had kept her mind occupied. She sat, idle, her whole mouth throbbing. Dr Grimes rose and picked up her chart again.

'All that work . . . ' He shook his head sorrowfully. 'Now, could you come in again tomorrow, we'll have to take some X-rays, see how far this thing has gone.'

'Will it mean false teeth?' she asked tremulously.

'Might do, hard to say.'

She tried to look crestfallen.

She went home in a state of excitement, her fat left cheek tingling faintly. She smiled at her reflection in the dark windows of the bus – a gormless, lopsided grin. Dentures! Soon these dying gums might house a complete set of beautiful, dazed teeth. A whole new smile. She would be able to take them out and watch them glistening in a glass of effervescent toothwash. Things of beauty in themselves. Dr Grimes was going to make a new woman of her. And she was going home to a houseful of strange men.

AGONY AUNT

Dear Marj,

I'm writing to you about my sister . . . let's call her
Mavis. That's not her real name, of course, but I've had
to change it, and some of the circumstances, in case she'd
recognise herself. Mavis has a problem; she's pregnant.
Not that this is a problem in itself, but, well . . . let me
start at the beginning.

Mavis is thirty-five. An elderly *prima gravida*. That's
what they called her at the hospital. She wasn't a bit
pleased. She doesn't like to be reminded of her age.
She's married, happily I've always thought, but then my
trouble is I always presume other people are happy. Ken
and Mavis. See, I think of them in the one breath. I was
sixteen when they married, a frumpy bridesmaid in peach
satin. Ken's a lovable dog of a man, the sort you'd miss if
he weren't around. He would never hurt Mavis. He's not
the kind to have passionate affairs. He would never walk
out on her. No, he's too loyal for that. Oh dear, that makes
him sound dull, doesn't it? And he's not dull, really; he's
genuinely kind in a dogged sort of way. He's served as a
sort of model for me. This, I thought, was what all men

were. It wasn't such a bad introduction, really. For many years I thought my life would run parallel to Mavis's, that I would meet and marry a man like Ken who would be utterly devoted to me. Now, of course, I'm not so sure. I've developed what Mavis calls an unsavoury taste in men. Meaning, I suppose, that there have been several lately. It's during discussions like these that our age difference shows – ten years, to be exact. A neat parenthesis of our parents' marriage. A desert in between.

I was surprised when Mavis talked about getting pregnant. I mean, she's never been the baby type. I'm much more gooey-eyed about them. I'm one of those women who can't let a pram go by without peering into it. I love to hold babies, drink up all that trust in their eyes. I love the way they wrap their little fingers round your thumb and their milky burps on your shoulder. And then later, how cute they are when they start to talk and have to have their fringes cut for the first time . . . see, I just can't stop. But Mavis, Mavis has always been embarrassed by children. Yes, embarrassed. She goes shy and tongue-tied when they're around. She wants them to be put to bed or taken away. I've seen her blush when toddlers ask those ridiculous questions like – what are those things? – pointing to your nipples. I find it hilarious; she *hates* it. She dreads the company of children. Too much of a child herself, she used to say. The funny thing is, I think she'd make a wonderful mother – or I used to. She has a practical, capable air which inspires confidence. She is big-boned and ample – for God's sake, she's looked like a mother for years. And Ken would dote on children. So, what's the problem? It's the way she talks about it. The longed-for baby. Oh yes, they were trying long enough. I thought these things were just a matter of timing and lust (though a lustful Ken is hard to imagine) or even, if necessary, a bout of manufactured desire. But it wasn't quite like that.

Imagine, the gynaecologist told Mavis, imagine your tubes to be like this. He stood up, a portly man, and raised his arms above his head like a belly dancer. He twiddled his fingers. These, he said, are your ovaries. Now, one of the tubes is blocked. He crooked his left arm, a circus clown feigning sadness. See? He sank back in his swivel chair. Women always identify with that, he said happily.

Her X-rays were clipped behind him on an illuminated screen.

'Fifty per cent chance of conceiving,' he said. 'Your age, of course . . . the biological clock, I suppose?'

This is an explanation that satisfies almost everyone. But for Mavis it wasn't that, although it *was* a matter of time. It was time for children, not because of a rush of broody hormones but because she had tired of being a child herself. If Mother died tomorrow, she said, I'd be nobody's child.

Trying for a baby. Something I imagined to be so easy in a slippery, lubricated way sounded instead dry and grating the way Mavis described it. It was as if a team of men with clipboards had moved in with them, timing and charting them, taking temperatures, counting days, extracting samples. It became, she said, nothing more than an absurd grappling, a fitting of parts together, square peg into round hole. This, she said to me once, is how prostitutes must feel. She and Ken would lie back afterwards, exhausted by the effort of coupling within the allotted time. She almost expected to see a row of judges walk into the bedroom carrying large white score cards – 7.6, 8.5, 9.4 . . . Must try harder.

Does it matter how we are conceived? I mean, we don't celebrate our conception as we do our birth, do we? Maybe because we know so little about it. Here is how I imagine mine – with Mavis's help, of course, she was there. Mother is in the kitchen. It is one of those taut, melancholy evenings in early spring. She is turning bread out on to a wire tray, tapping the floury bottoms of the loaves, humming softly to herself. I imagine the large airy kitchen that Mavis describes in the old house which we left after Father died. I hear the drone of a lawnmower, the booming of a radio. Mavis, with red pigtails, legs thrown wide, arches her back and swoops on a makeshift tree swing at the end of the garden. Suddenly, there is an intruder, a man who must be Father. I don't remember him. I discovered an old photograph of him once. It showed a group of men in a high-walled yard, three in soldiers' uniforms with rifles cocked at a man with a blindfold; beside him a cassocked priest reading from a bible. It was a mock-up, my mother said, they dressed up for the camera. The memory of civil war was still fresh then, she said. Father was the man about to be executed. It is this man, desperate and on the run, who blunders into the kitchen.

Mother has only time to look around momentarily before he grabs her from behind. He catches the stuff of her dress in his fist and yanks her towards him, his face shiny with anger. He tears the cloth from neck to shoulder; it hangs off her like a flap of skin. He pushes her against the wall. She slithers, grasping at the counter and upsetting a vase of daffodils which crashes to the floor in a shocking temper. She struggles to rise but he pushes her down, pinioning her. She beats him around the neck with her free hand. He catches it and holds it down against the floor. Her hair is bathed in a pool of water; the broken stalks of daffodils are strewn by her head. He crushes her cheek on a jagged shard. She still has the scar – a crescent on her cheekbone. He catches her hair and pulls it away from her face. He spits on her. She wriggles one arm free and strikes him across the mouth. She draws blood. He sits down on her, tears down her knickers, unzips and enters.

'Bitch,' he hisses at her, 'bitch!'

In the garden, Mavis tumbles from the swing.

In the early months, anything global frightened her. The

possibility of nuclear accident, tidal waves, any kind of natural disaster. Even spring coming early. There were daffodils in January, crocuses too. The cherry blossom was in flower by Ash Wednesday. The mild, clammy winter gave way to wild fits of temper, nights bullied by gales. The snowdrops were whipped and broken as if in punishment for coming out too soon. Trees keeled over. Global warming, Mavis said, the greenhouse effect. Imagine, she said, all those carbon dioxide fumes belching into the earth's atmosphere, eating away at the ozone layer. I suppose there wasn't anything unusual about all of this. I mean, don't all mothers-to-be become haunted by the world they are about to deliver into? She gave up work. *That* reassured me. I took it as absolute proof of her devotion. I'd never known Mavis not to work; it was what big sisters did. But her fears grew once she was at home all day. She brooded about droughts and famines, the spreading deserts, the felling of rain forests. She talked of the vast upset of oceans and atmospheres as if – I know this sounds crazy – as if the fact of her pregnancy had set all of these things in motion, as if the world had suddenly turned on her, venomous and hostile.

Perhaps I expected too much of Mavis. I admit I'm over-reverent about motherhood. The pain of it, mostly, the great searing pain of physical rupture. And I envy women who have had babies, not just for the angelic creatures they produce, but because it seems to give them such powers. They come into an instinct that makes them

wise and protective, which alerts them instantly when
their child is in danger. They *know* without ever having
been taught. But this is probably all fanciful tosh. I don't
think any of this when I see pale, undernourished women
in the city, six or seven months gone, dark circles under
their eyes, their hands clutching the small of their backs,
carrying this huge globe ahead of them as if they truly
had the weight of the world girded around them. *They
look as if their spines, like stalks, might snap.*

At five months Mavis went missing. Just for a few hours,
but it was enough to scare us, Ken and I, that is. Mother
never knew. Ken came home one Friday evening to find
a note from her saying she'd be back in a few days. He
was frantic. He called around to me.

'Where could she possibly have gone?' he asked me.
'*You* should know.' He said this with untypical rancour.
Mavis and I have always been close; sometimes she tells
me things that perhaps I shouldn't know like all that
intimate stuff when they were trying for the baby. But
Ken needn't have worried; she's never talked about what
she feels for him; what I hear are the nuts and bolts of
it.

'I've no idea,' I said. But, of course, I had my suspicions.
The legal limit is 24 weeks.

'This is most unlike her,' Ken said.

But was it? Once, yes, but now anything seemed
possible and that included Ken getting angry. Our Ken!

'If you know anything . . . ' He wagged a finger at me; that was the closest he would come to menace.

'I'd tell you, honestly, Ken, I would.'

But would I have? In the event it didn't matter because she turned up close to midnight. There was no explanation, or if there was, I didn't get to hear of it. There is an expression of Mavis's, a sort of closed-down look, a set to her mouth, a crease between her eyebrows, when no challenges will be brooked. I'd seen it many times when I was younger and would crash into her room, ripe with news or weary with boredom. Usually her friends would be there, drinking coffee, smoking and talking with a lazy kind of animation which stopped abruptly when I entered. These big girls had a secret language, I was sure, a way of looking at one another heavy with meaning from which I would be forever excluded. There was something compelling about the way they worked together, bending over their compacts or zipping one another into spangly dresses. I would have been quite happy to slide into a corner and just watch as Lily, lying on the bed, rolled herself into a pair of jeans or Greta, brandishing lipstick, closed her eyes and pocked her mouth in a mockery of ecstasy. But Mavis wouldn't have it. She'd turn on me and glare in that way that said – keep out. The others didn't see it. She was careful of the people she shut out. Ken knows that expression too, I'm sure. It is, I suspect, how she looked when she returned after those lost hours of hers.

'You know the optimum age for childbirth?' Mavis asked
me the other day. She's seven-and-a-half months gone
now. I said nothing. All of Mavis's questions these days
are traps.

'Eighteen to twenty-three when the body is still tight,
shiny, new.' She patted the bump disparagingly. 'Mine
is a rotting house. Draughty, tampered with.'

She heaved herself up from the table. She is uncomfortable now – the heat makes her breathy and glistening.

'There's a forced plant in here, it's blossoming too
brightly. See how big it is?' She looked at me with dour
satisfaction.

'Maybe it's due earlier than you think. Maybe your
dates are wrong?'

'You think I don't remember when it was conceived?
I could practically put a stopwatch on it.'

'Mavis, can I ask you something?'

'Oh sure, the font of all knowledge here.' She smiled
at me in a strange, savage way.

'Don't you want this baby?'

She sank into a chair looking suddenly defeated.

'I can't not want it now, can I?'

'But you *do* want it, don't you?'

'I want to be what I was. Alone, special. I can't
ever be that again.'

She wiped her brow with the back of her hand.

'Oh, when we were trying it seemed vital to be
pregnant because it was so difficult and because other

people had babies so easily. I'm having this to prove I could.'

She laughed with a downturn of her lip.

'Not much of a reason to have a child.'

'But you'll love it when it comes, it'll be different then.'

'You think so?' She stared at me, tearfully defiant.

'Of course you will, it's what happens. Remember what Mother used to always say about me, how difficult things were, what with Father and all, and yet how welcome I was, don't you remember?'

'Oh yes,' she said, 'I remember all right. There was a great fuss made of you.'

'And see, everything turned out all right, didn't it?'

And then I remembered another fragment, one of Mother's reminiscences. She has a dreamy way of remembering, lapsing into half-thought, half-talk so that afterwards it is difficult to distinguish between things she has told me and things I remember myself. In this memory she is on the landing of the old house. She is moving carefully down the strip of plum-coloured carpet which stretches to the head of the stairs. She is carrying a tea tray.

'Your late father was sick then,' she said, 'and I was almost ready to pop with you.'

She had just reached the top of the stairs, she said, and was thinking she should turn the light on because in the dimness she could barely see where she was going.

'That was such a gloomy house, big old barn of a place.'

Mavis was coming out of her room and Mother called to her over her shoulder.

'Mavis, darling, run and turn the light on, would you?'

She heard the click as Mavis shut the door of her room behind her.

'Mavis?'

Mother turned around. Mavis stood there, stony-faced. She had a doll in her hand, a rag-doll she had been fond of when she'd been younger. She had the doll by the hair and she trailed it along behind her as she came towards Mother.

'Please, Mavis, help Mummy out now, there's a good girl. I can't see where I'm going.'

Mavis sidled up to her in the gloom but made no move towards the switch.

'I was scared,' Mother told me, 'isn't that ridiculous? A grown woman scared of a ten-year old?' She laughed nervously.

'The light, Mavis, *please!*'

And then, quite casually, Mavis pushed her. It was the tray that fell. It bounced and clattered down the stairs, cups flying, the quick flash of knives. Mother clutched the banister to steady herself.

'Your balance goes,' she said to me, 'carrying all that weight around.'

She took my hand in hers and rubbed my fingers thoughtfully with her thumb.

'Mavis looked as if she might kill me that day.' She

paused. 'But I think it was you she was after . . . '

I like the idea of being an auntie, although I'm not one yet, I suppose, technically speaking. But I *feel* I am. Already I'm looking at clothes for three-year-olds and planning excursions for when she can walk and talk. It will be a girl, I'm sure. The first of the next generation. Yes, there *is* something special about first-borns. Ken is getting excited too. He's decorating the boxroom. The window is wide open to allow the paint to dry. I can hear him whistling as he works. Mother is knitting – matinee jackets and mittens in yellow and knicker pink. She is apprehensive about the birth. Mavis is the same age as she was when she had me and I was a difficult one. She worries that Mavis isn't ready. By this she means that Mavis hasn't gathered up all the necessary material things to greet the new arrival – baby bath, cot, buggy etc. She's right. Mavis isn't ready. I see her now sitting in the shade of the garden, sluggish and limp, sunk in a kind of torpor like someone condemned. I'm afraid sometimes that she might do herself damage, you know, something awful with a clothes hanger, and then I chide myself for even thinking such a thing. She wouldn't, would she? Trouble is, I don't know anymore – if I ever did – what Mavis would or wouldn't do. That's why I'm writing to you, though I don't know if I'll post this in the end. Under normal circumstances I wouldn't dream of doing such a thing, spilling out my – I mean, our –

private life to a complete stranger, but I've no one left to turn to. What good is family at a time like this?

Yours,

A CURSE

A WOMAN STOOPS in a darkened room. It is a nursery, but underfurnished. There is a cot and a chest of drawers and the smell of newly-laid carpet. The curtains are drawn but it is daylight outside. She has just put the baby down. There is, miraculously, perfect silence save for the child's noisy, congested breathing that is not quite regular enough for Clara to feel at ease. The baby has been crying for days. Since she arrived, in fact. Eight days ago when the social worker handed her over. She has an angry rash on her face and scratches from her own small, sharp nails. Colicky, the doctor says, a colicky baby. Clara thinks she has soothed her into sleep. She has been pacing the house with the baby on her shoulder for several hours. She has got to know fragments of it in a hypnotic sort of way. She has noticed, for instance, how smooth the polished knob at the end of the banisters is and the gold work around the mirror in the hall. Door handles seem suddenly impossibly intricate. She has used them for measuring – when I pass this point again she will be asleep. Yesterday Clara did 57 rounds of the house. Gingerly she straightens up. The baby still has hold of her finger, lightly trapped in her fist. If she can extricate it without the baby noticing, there will be peace. There have been eight days of bargains like this. Clara inches her finger free. She has suddenly become aware of each tiny movement of her own, and how crude and overstated the gestures of the adult world are. The baby stirs, making a gnawing sound in her throat. Clara is about to turn away when there is a little whimper. She dashes clumsily for the door . . . if she is out of the room before . . . but by the time she reaches it the baby is howling. She feels tears of rage springing to her eyes. She lunges at the cot and picks the baby up roughly. She shakes her and shakes her, screaming at the child. Her own voice, when she finally hears it, shrill and savage, frightens her into a numbed silence. And then she remembers the curse. A baby, not her own, and the desire for revenge.

Theirs was a dead house, the atmosphere petrified into something heavy and dark. She imagined it to be the expelled air of her father's lungs still trapped in the house. He had breathed his last in the room upstairs. He had made practically everything with his own hands – the kitchen table, the bookshelves, the armchairs, the wardrobes – but as the months went by she noticed how these things were being drained of their ownership. They were no longer the things that Daddy had made, they were just things to sit on and use. Soon she would look at them and not find them special in any way at all. The house made her restless, the silence driving her from room to room as if in search of something she had misplaced.

Her other world was the Skerritts where she babysat at weekends. They lived on an estate on the Mellick Road in a house, which although new, was already battered-looking. The window frames were warped and when it rained large bed-wetter's stains appeared on the gable. Shoddy workmanship, her father had said. Inside it had been sabotaged at child-level. The wallpaper had been picked off at the seams, the skirting-boards were scuffed, cupboard doors gaped open to reveal a jumble of entrails. And yet, there was something cheerful and optimistic about the Skerritts' dishevelled kitchen with daubed paintings by Marcus on the walls and the linoleum littered with building blocks and plastic toys that squawked when you stood on them unwittingly. Their sideboard in the dining-room had only enough history to house a single set of crystal glasses; there were bare rooms upstairs stacked high with tea-chests as if the Skerritts hadn't fully taken possession.

The surfaces of melamine and veneer spoke to Clara of newness and modernity; *this* was the kind of house she would live in when she grew up and Mr Skerritt, rakish and affable, the sort of man she imagined marrying.

'And how's our Clara?' he would ask jovially, opening the hall door. He was a large, bulky man with a thatch of coarse brown hair and a pleasant, weary face. He would show Clara into the sitting-room with a mocking flourish and while Mrs Skerritt finished getting ready upstairs he would sit down and hazard conversation with her. He settled on the armchair as if it were an unbroken horse that might at any moment throw him, his hands clamped tenaciously on its flanks. He constantly shifted around rolling his shoulders as if something in his back was getting crushed.

'How's school?' he always asked.

She would shrug.

'Other things on your mind, eh?' He would wink broadly. 'Any boyfriends yet?'

She would look away.

'Aha, I see, not telling. We're expecting to come home some night and find a young blade here, isn't that right, Joy?'

Mrs Skerritt would walk in on a wave of heavy perfume. She wore extravagant spangly dresses, off-the-shoulder styles which showed up the fragile bones around her neck. Clara envied her slenderness. 'I should hope not,' she would say severely to him, and to Clara: 'Marcus is asleep but he may wake later, he's teething.'

'Just knock him out with the bottled dope,' he would interject.

'Denis, *please*! . . . I've left you out some supper. There's milk, biscuits, you know where everything is.'

'Are we ready then?' he would ask slapping the arms of the chair heartily as he rose.

'How do I look?' she would ask peering at herself anxiously in the mirror over the mantelpiece.

'Smashing, eh Clara?'

Clara would nod firmly.

'We may be late . . . ' Mrs Skerritt's face would crease worriedly. 'I've left a number by the phone just in case . . . '

'C'mon, C'mon,' he would say, whacking Joy on the thigh, 'let's leave this young one to it.' And he would leave with one last broad wink.

She waited until she heard the car reverse and head off with a throaty roar before she settled in – throwing the cushions from the sofa on to the floor, turning the television on, kicking off her shoes and sprawling on the carpet. She made coffee which they didn't have at home. It was easier here to imagine herself as an extension of the television world she watched so avidly. A world of bungalows, station wagons in the driveway, boys on bicycles firing newspapers at doorsteps, milkshakes, diners, donuts, drive-in movies, beer in the fridge, high-school proms, the racket of cicadas on a summer's night, the whine and slam of a screen door . . .

She explored every inch of the Skerritts' house. Their bedroom had all the abandon of a shared intimate life. A tousled double bed with clothes dripping off the end and trailing onto the floor. It had a cushioned headboard and was so fat and low that when she lay on it she could hang her arm out over the edge and touch the floor with her fingers. There were speckles of talc on the dark carpet. Nests of beads were strung around the mirror; a city of creams on the dressing-table. There was usually a fat paperback lying face down on the pillow. The room seemed always about to yield up its adult secrets but she was afraid to stay in it too long in case she would be caught. She knew that it was out of bounds.

The bathroom, too, seemed sensual with its potent mix of male and female. It had pink carpet which lapped up the side of the bath and made the room seem like a tilted ship. It did not smell of antiseptic and spearmint toothpaste, as the bathroom at home did, where everything was locked away in a cabinet over the basin. Here, shaving foam and cotton buds, razors, hair clips, shampoo, hair oil, comb and shower cap were all shamelessly on display. A man's dressing-gown was slewed over the side of the bath, a pair of stricken nylons abandoned by the door.

Her greatest fear was that Marcus would die quietly in the night, so much so that each time she checked on him she would have to walk right into his room and put her head close down to his face to make sure he was breathing. She would put her palm on his forehead and run her fingers through his dampish hair. He would shift slightly at the touch and make small, grinding noises with his teeth. Clara felt hers was a fitting pose. It spoke of care and expertise; it was, she thought, what mothers did.

The Skerritts sometimes went to dinner dances which kept them out until the early hours. On those nights, Clara usually stayed over. After midnight, drugged by a night of livid-blue TV, she found the silence of the house terrifying. Even the ticking of a clock seemed monstrous.

She would lie awake in the spare room waiting for the sound of the key in the door and the reassurance of adult voices. Sometimes she would hear a truncated giggle on the stairway as they made their way to bed, or the murmur of talk in the next room. If she hadn't gone to bed, Mr Skerritt would run her home. Their car smelt of pine needles. His breath bore the sweet tang of alcohol. He was always quieter then, less jaunty than earlier and they usually travelled in silence. He would turn the car radio up and on summer nights he would wind the window down on his side. The breeze ruffling through her hair, the bleating of the music, a man sitting next to her, this was what Clara knew of love. She imagined them as parties to a secret, she and Mr Skerritt, as if driving in the dark together was some kind of forbidden pleasure. And when he dropped her off he often slipped her an extra pound as if, indeed, they had shared something illicit in the night.

Clara's mother would usually be asleep by the time she got home. She had never met the Skerritts; they were just voices on the phone to her and that was the way Clara wanted to keep it. She considered Denis and Joy (that's what she called them to herself though never to their faces) and Marcus too, as her private property, a world apart. But her mother was curious about them.

'They do a lot of gadding about,' she said to Clara, 'for a married couple.'

'No reason why they shouldn't enjoy themselves, is there?'

'No need to get uppity, my girl. All I'm saying is that it wasn't like that in our day. You scrimped and saved and stayed at home. When your father and I got married first we . . . '

Clara rose abruptly and started to clear the dishes noisily. She panicked when her mother talked like this; she wanted to hear none of it. She knew that in mid-story her mother's face would cloud over and she would lapse into a silence which to Clara seemed full of recrimination. There were never tears, just an accusing kind of gloom.

The year Clara turned fifteen, Joy Skerritt fell pregnant for the second time. Fallen; she toyed with the words that adults used. It was Mr Skerritt who told her one night as he drove her home.

'We could have done without it,' he said. 'How and ever, we shall be needing you all the more when number two arrives.'

He smiled at her and squeezed her hand.

'We *do* depend on you, you know.'

She flushed, feeling that some privilege had been conferred on her. That night Mr Skerritt forgot to pay her altogether.

It was a hot summer, long days of unforgiving heat. Sometimes during the week Mrs Skerritt would ring and ask Clara to come around and look after Marcus in the daytime while she rested. Clara was glad of the chance to escape from home. The house seemed even more shut-up in the heat. Her father's dark furniture seemed to absorb all the light and the rooms were stuffy. Joy looked like a large, ungainly ship. She walked as if the air around her was heavy. She clutched her back with one hand and her forehead with the other and exhaled deeply.

'This heat is killing me.'

Clara thought of Mrs Skerritt's wardrobe upstairs which she had riffled through many times, the splashy silks and beaded bouclés, and wondered if they would ever be worn again. *That* Joy Skerritt seemed to have been entirely subsumed.

Clara, in a T-shirt and shorts, took Marcus's hand.

'Let's go to the park, shall we?'

Joy Skerritt retreated to her cool, darkened room.

She and Marcus spent several hours in the park. The sun beat down as she lolled on a bench and Marcus, in a sea of toddlers, clambered on the play frame and careered joyously down the slide. She was suddenly proud of him – his knack of being happy and tirelessly occupied like this – as proud, she imagined, as if he had been her own child. By the time they got home it was nearing six. She could feel the skin of her face tightening from the hours in the heat.

Mr Skerritt was in the kitchen. Joy was nowhere to be seen.

'Well, well, well, home is the hunter! And how's my little horror today?'

He swept a squealing Marcus up in his arms. 'Not

forgetting the paid help.' He shot a sly smile in her direction.

'My, my,' he added, 'don't you look well, you look as if you've got the sun.'

When she got home Clara went straight to her room. She locked the door and undressed in front of the long mirror set into the wardrobe door. What she saw did not please her. She had got the sun all right; it had left a red high-tide mark on her arms and at her neck as if she were permanently embarrassed. She scowled at her puffy breasts, the dark tufts of hair between her legs, her drooping shoulders. It was the sort of body a man might call voluptuous – if there were a man. But, she thought, just now I am prettier than Joy.

The afternoon she was taken into hospital, Mr Skerritt rang Clara and asked her to stay overnight. When she arrived at the house, Joy, huge and afraid, sat perched on a chair in the hall; a tousled Marcus leaning against her, his head in her lap. Mr Skerritt rushed from the kitchen.

'Thank God you're here, Clara,' he said. 'It's coming early . . . c'mon, Joy.' He helped to heave her up. Marcus clung to her and started to cry.

'There, there, my pet, Clara's going to look after you, aren't you Clara? Mummy must go to the hospital to get the new baby . . . '

'Want to go with you,' he wailed.

'Oh, Marcus, don't be a baby,' Mr Skerritt barked.

'They don't let children in, darling.'

'Clara . . . would you?' Mr Skerritt said irritably to her as if she should know what to do.

Clara took Marcus's hand. He grabbed it away and slapped her on the stomach but nobody saw. It would always be the same, she thought. She had cleaned and looked after Marcus since he was a baby, yet he would never love her; he would never even be loyal to her; he would always prefer Joy.

Denis and Joy lumbered towards the open door.

'He'll be all right once we're gone,' Mr Skerritt said over his shoulder.

As soon as they stepped outside, he banged the door. Marcus ran after them beating his fists against it and screaming. Clara left him there. He could cry all he liked as far as she was concerned.

A half-hour later he trudged into the sitting room where she had turned on the television. She hadn't been watching it, at least not properly. She had paced up and down feeling guilty and cruel, going to the door from time to time and checking to see if he was all right. But she didn't want him to know that. She wanted him to think she didn't care. He came over to her, his face blotchy, his tears subsided into soft little shudders, and climbed on her.

'Plenty room on my lap,' she said to him.

By seven she had given him his tea and he was in bed. The night stretched ahead endlessly. A mountain of crinkled washing, fresh from the line, had been dumped on the kitchen table. She took out the ironing board and worked for several hours, back and forth, taking special care with the creases on Mr Skerritt's shirts.

'He has to be immaculate for work,' Joy had told her.

Clara remembered everything Joy said about Mr Skerritt; from her she would learn what pleased men. She carried the stacks of neat laundry upstairs and arranged them in the hot press. Joy put her towels on the middle rack, Clara noticed, but she felt they would be better up high and moved them, replacing them with Mr Skerritt's shirts. She wanted to be sure he would notice them.

She cleaned the kitchen. There were stacks of dirty dishes and saucepans with muddy-coloured rings inside. The stove had burnt-in food around the rings. The grill was caked with grease. Joy had really let herself go these past few days, Clara thought. She felt sure Mr Skerritt could not be happy coming home to a house in this state.

By 10.30 the place was gleaming and Clara, cup of coffee in hand, settled in front of the television hoping she looked as if she had been sitting there all evening. She would not have wanted Mr Skerritt coming upon her as she scoured in the oven, to see her flushed and sweaty, her sleeves rolled up, her hair in a state. No, this was the way she wanted it to be. The warm house, the sleeping child, the man about to come home, and she as the woman waiting.

'It's a girl!' he said bursting through the door of the sitting-room. Clara must have dropped off. There was a high-pitched pinging from the blank television and a damp spot on her blouse where she must have dribbled in her sleep. Her mouth tasted sour. She roused herself.

'That's great,' she said and immediately felt it sounded lame. She heard her voice like this sometimes, hollow and monotonous, as if she was convinced of nothing she said, as if nothing moved or excited her. 'How's Mrs Skerritt?'

He pulled a face.

'A bit rough, it was a long labour, nearly twelve hours. She's pretty exhausted and then there's the stitches but the baby is fine, thank God. You should see her, a great mop of dark hair and the most beautiful long fingers, just like Joy's. We're going to call her Rose, did we tell you?'

'Oh, that's lovely.'

A silence fell.

'After Joy's mother . . . crusty old bitch. Oops, pardon the French. Don't tell her I said that, will you?' He looked across at her apprehensively.

'No, I won't.'

'Swear?'

'I swear,' she said solemnly.

'Did you know,' he said rising to pour himself a drink, 'that, originally, swearing in court was a way of cursing yourself? If you didn't tell the truth you were literally wishing badness on yourself.'

Clara shook her head.

'I tell my clients that to frighten them. Well, no, not to frighten them, but to warn them that things have a habit of coming back at you.'

He sat down and loosened his tie.

'Sooner or later, we all have to pay.'

She slept in Marcus's room. She liked its gayness, the posters and the mobiles, its feeling of clutter. She woke early. Bright morning sunshine streamed into the room. She could hear Mr Skerritt moving about. It was only a short walk across the landing to his room where the door was always left ajar. Marcus was rattling the bars of the cot. She brought him downstairs and put him in the high chair while she prepared his porridge and put the coffee pot on. Denis liked coffee in the mornings, Joy had told her. She debated on whether to bring him up a tray but she thought better of it. Who knew what she might find? He might not wear pyjamas or she might catch him half-dressed. She padded to the fridge to get milk. The door was dotted with magnetic fruit – strawberries, pineapples and bananas – under which wads of notes and messages were pinned. 'Ring dentist,' said one. 'Cleaners, collect Thurs,' said another with a torn-off stub stuck with it. 'Money for Clara?' This last was written in Mr Skerritt's hand. Clara blushed. It sounded, to her, like the kind of wistful declaration that would come at the end of a love letter.

'Doesn't he drive you mad?' he asked her that morning,

nodding to Marcus who was wandering around the kitchen in search of something to grab hold of and bring tottering down.

'It's what I'm paid for,' she said pouring him his coffee. She had meant to sound bright and willing; instead she sounded sullen. She sat down opposite him and watched him as he ate. She was both grateful for and embarrassed by this sudden show of curiosity about her.

'Ah, yes, but there must be loads of other things you'd rather be doing . . . There must be boys.'

She shook her head.

'Come, come, a fine girl like you . . . '

She said nothing. This kindly tone made her uneasy; she preferred him when he was joking.

'Ah well, all I can say is they must be blind . . . isn't that right, Marcus?'

Marcus beamed.

'See? Marcus agrees with me.'

For the moment that he stood there with his arm around his son, and both of them gazing at her, Clara was absurdly happy.

She remembered those days as airy and laden with sound. Shafts of dusty sunlight flooding into bleached rooms. The whine of a chainsaw, the aggravated squawk of a swing, the sound of doors slamming in the draughts of a house thrown open to the sun. Mr Skerritt snoring on a kitchen chair placed on paving concrete outside the back door, the newspaper over his face. He always woke with a start, snorting like a horse and thrashing at the paper as if it were trying to throttle him. He was often no more than a disembodied presence, a voice calling out in the hallway, a jacket thrown over the banisters. Or she would hear him whistling in some other room, in sharp, disjointed phrases which stopped abruptly halfway through, only to be followed minutes later by another burst in a higher pitch. In fact, sometimes, Clara preferred the idea of his proximity and the imminence of his arrival to his actual presence. That way it was easier to keep intact the notion that this was her life now. It was only when she came across evidence of his shared life with Joy that she felt twinges of envy – his keys nestling in her scarf on the hall table, her underwear among his shirts in the laundry – because these things held within them the certainty of continuing. And she knew sooner or later Joy would come home.

The morning she was due home, Clara and Mr Skerritt took the house by storm. The kitchen floor was swept and Marcus's toys which had lain around for days were tidied away into a box which was then shoved unceremoniously into the cupboard under the stairs. Mr Skerritt cleaned their bedroom. Clara could hear him nosing into the corners with the vacuum cleaner and knocking up against the furniture as she tackled a wash-up downstairs.

'What a mess!' he said when he re-emerged. 'Joy has only to be gone for a few days and I revert to my bachelor ways, I'm afraid.' He surveyed the kitchen.

'By God, she won't know the place . . . '

Clara, wiping down the draining board, felt a sudden pang. All this was for Joy; soon, *she* would no longer be needed; soon, she would be shut out again.

'You know, Clara, you're a treasure. I don't know what I'd have done without you these past few days.'

He put his arm around her shoulder and gave her a friendly squeeze.

Suddenly, unbidden, there were tears in her eyes. She buried her head in his chest so he wouldn't notice. Gently, he stroked her head.

'There, there,' he said.

She found herself crying silently, biting her lip to keep the sobs from escaping, her hands clutching the stuff of his shirt in gnarled bunches. Afterwards, she couldn't remember how long they had stood like this, but finally from what seemed a long way off, the phone rang. He pulled away and went to answer it.

'Sweetheart!' she heard him say, 'yes, yes, I'm on my way . . . '

Clara fled to the bathroom.

Rose's christening was in September.

'We're having thirty in,' Mrs Skerritt said on the phone, 'so I could do with a hand. Maybe you'd help me serve and keep Marcus out of our hair?' Clara didn't want to go but she couldn't say that. Joy took her silence for assent.

'We'll see you at eleven on Saturday, then?'

She had not been at the Skerritts since the day Joy had come home from the hospital and she had secretly hoped that they had found another babysitter. But why would they do that? To Joy, Clara was the good, sensible girl she had always been. Only Mr Skerritt knew differently.

The house was in chaos when she arrived. Marcus was screaming in the hall. Joy was upstairs changing the baby and Mr Skerritt was at the kitchen table with a basin of potato peels in front of him.

'For the salad,' he said.

She remembered with a blush what had happened in this room – with him. But she could tell that he wasn't in the slightest embarrassed about it. Maybe this sort of thing meant nothing to adults.

'Can I help?' she asked.

'Oh, could you? Tell you what, you take over here and I'll go and see if I can quieten Marcus down.'

He rose from the table and handed Clara the knife.

'He's wild jealous of the new baby.'

Everything, Clara noticed, had returned to normal. Joy, wearing a kaftan swept into the kitchen. She had large, lavish earrings and a pair of bangles jangling at her wrist.

'Do I look huge in this?' she asked.

'You look a million dollars, doesn't she, Clara?'

'Yes,' Clara said and went back to her peelings.

They laid the food out on a trestle table near the French window, covering it with a cloth so the wasps wouldn't get at it.

'They're dying at the moment,' Clara heard Mr Skerritt say to Marcus, 'their stings are at their worst now.'

In her absence, Marcus had got taller. He looked less of a baby now. His face had got thin, his limbs longer. Clara was sure he didn't remember her. Or, if he did, he remembered that day when she had let him cry himself out in the hallway with no one to comfort him.

The ceremony was at one. Clara wasn't invited although she'd worn her good dress just in case. But no, she thought sourly, I'm only good enough to watch the pots at home. And to mind Marcus, though in the end he threw such a tantrum that Joy said pleadingly; 'Ah, let him come.'

'Anything for a quiet life,' Mr Skerritt said whisking the new baby out to the car. All Clara saw of her was the long white tail of the christening robe. She didn't want to see any more. In some way, she associated Rose with all her own feelings of ill-luck and humiliation. If there hadn't been a second baby, none of this with Mr Skerritt would have happened.

After an hour, the front door opened and a triumphant flood of conversation entered the house. They were mostly relations, some neighbours, and a gaggle of women who were friends of Joy's from college. Clara served them wine, weaving in and out between the little knots of

people as they scattered across the scorched lawn. It was
a wistful kind of day. A haze hung over the garden but
there was a chill in the breeze and it was cool in the
shadows. After the first drinks were served, Mrs Skerritt
motioned to Clara to uncover the food. The guests milled
around the table gathering cutlery – it was a running buffet
– tottering away afterwards with precariously loaded paper
plates and glasses hugged to their bodies. Clara did several
more rounds with the wine. No one took any notice of
her – oh, they smiled and nodded gratefully to her when
she filled their glasses but otherwise she might as well not
have existed. And Marcus, supposedly her charge for the
day, was asleep in his granny's lap, spent from his earlier
temper. Clara retreated to the kitchen with a tray of empty
glasses. Her feet ached. She sat down, glad of the deserted
room. The windows were open and she could hear the
quiet murmur of conversation from outside.

'That's a great girl you have helping out, Joy,' one of
the voices said. Joy, coming closer, said: 'Yes, she's a real
find . . . although there was a bit of trouble when I was
in having Rose . . . '

'Oh, really?'

'Denis will tell you *all*.'

Clara sunk lower into her chair.

'Ah well, you know how it is at that age,' Mr
Skerritt said.

Somebody giggled.

'You mean she's got a crush on you, Denis, is that it?'

More peals of laughter.

'Well, I did warn you, Denis,' Joy said. 'I saw it coming a mile off. Those quiet types harbour all sorts of yearnings.'

'It's not like that, Joy, really. She's just lost her father and well, I feel sorry for her, that's all.'

'There was a scene here while I was away,' she heard Joy say, 'so we decided to ease off for a while, give her time to get over it. It seems fine now, don't you think, Denis?'

He didn't answer.

She had to get out. She stood up, her hands clenched around the tea-towel she'd been holding in her lap. But she couldn't go, just like that, without an explanation. But how could she face them again? Her face was flushed and she knew if anyone spoke to her she would cry. She went upstairs to the bathroom, locked the door and leaned against it. A few hot, angry tears rolled down her cheek; the rest of them were trapped in a knot at her breastbone or drowning in her throat.

She heard someone coming up the stairs. The door handle was tried and there was a polite knock.

'Is there somebody in there?' the voice from outside called.

Hurriedly, Clara threw cold water on her blotchy face and wiped it vigorously with a towel. She opened the door boldly, startling the guest who was waiting outside.

'Sorry,' the woman said.

Clara scurried down the landing and into the baby's
room. Rose was asleep in a carry-cot which had been
left on the bed. The room was in darkness. Mrs Skerritt
had turned the blinds down to fool the baby into thinking
it was night. It had worked. Her breathing was regular,
her two little fists gathered at her mouth. Clara swept the
baby up in her arms. Rose's face screwed up into an angry
little knot. She opened her eyes, rubbing her nose crossly
with her gnarled fingers, her forehead creased into a dazed
frown. Clara laid her down on the bedspread and began to
undo the layers of clothes – the yellow blanket, the white
frilly christening robe, the hand-me-down babygro – until
Rose was down to her skin. It felt silky to Clara's touch.
Imagine, she thought, Rose has never felt the slightest
edge of a breeze. The thought gave her a pleasant, icy
chill. She undid the baby's nappy. Rose was wriggling
now, weaving her fists in the air. Clara looked down at
her spitefully. She hated this ugly little creature, her scaly
hands, her wizened face. She hated the careless parents
who left her alone while they partied downstairs. She
hated the way they had talked about her, the knowing
way Joy had scoffed. But what she hated most was Denis's
kindness. Because it was *only* kindness he was offering,
as compensation for such things as a dead father and her
age which was somehow unfortunate. And Clara wanted
more, much more than kindnesses. She caught up one of
the nappy pins and drove it directly into the baby's hip.
Rose screamed. Clara had drawn blood.

'There,' she said, 'that'll teach you.'

She picked Rose up and deposited her back in the carry-cot. She was roaring now, thin, angry cries. She was completely naked but there wasn't time to dress her. Somebody was bound to hear her crying. Clara hurriedly covered her up and ran from the room, shutting the door on the piercing cries. She took the stairs two at a time. Luckily, she met nobody. She halted as she opened the front door to take a last look; she had been happy here, after all. But, as she fled, she knew there would be a punishment for this. There was a curse on her now.